"Scoot a little closer, darlin'," Andrew said.

"I'm comfortable, thank you," Margaret Leigh murmured.

"For me?" He gave her a heart-tugging smile. "My reputation'll be ruined if folks see me driving down the street with all this room between me and my date." He looked so innocent, she gave in and moved closer.

"That's better." He slid his arm along the back of the seat and draped it over her shoulders. She'd never known a man's arm could feel so alive. "Don't you think that's better?"

"Well . . . it's closer."

Andrew laughed. "You're a treat, Margaret Leigh. I like a woman who speaks her mind and tells me the truth, instead of playing word games and saying what she thinks I want to hear."

She smiled. "My, you are a puzzle, Andrew McGill."

He turned toward her, and his face was solemn and tender. "Solve me. . . ."

WHAT ARE *LOVESWEPT* ROMANCES?

They are stories of true romance and touching emotion. We believe those two very important ingredients are constants in our highly sensual and very believable stories in the *LOVESWEPT* line. Our goal is to give you, the reader, stories of consistently high quality that may sometimes make you laugh, sometimes make you cry, but are always fresh and creative and contain many delightful surprises within their pages.

Most romance fans read an enormous number of books. Those they truly love, they keep. Others may be traded with friends and soon forgotten. We hope that each *LOVESWEPT* romance will be a treasure—a "keeper." We will always try to publish

LOVE STORIES YOU'LL NEVER FORGET
BY AUTHORS YOU'LL ALWAYS REMEMBER

The Editors

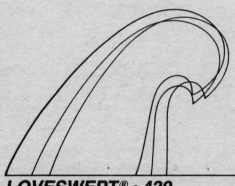

LOVESWEPT® • 439

Peggy Webb
Saturday Mornings

 BANTAM BOOKS
NEW YORK • TORONTO • LONDON • SYDNEY • AUCKLAND

SATURDAY MORNINGS
A Bantam Book / December 1990

If you would be interested in receiving protective vinyl covers for your Loveswept books, please write to this address for information:

Loveswept
Bantam Books
P. O. Box 985
Hicksville, NY 11802

ISBN 0-553-44070-5

Published simultaneously in the United States and Canada

Bantam Books are published by Bantam Books, a division of Bantam Doubleday Dell Publishing Group, Inc. Its trademark, consisting of the words "Bantam Books" and the portrayal of a rooster, is Registered in U.S. Patent and Trademark Office and in other countries. Marca Registrada. Bantam Books, 666 Fifth Avenue, New York, New York 10103.

PRINTED IN THE UNITED STATES OF AMERICA

OPM   0   9   8   7   6   5   4   3   2   1

Prologue

"Margaret Leigh, this poodle wet the rug again."

Margaret Leigh put her purse on the hall table, hung her blazer in the hall closet, and carefully tucked a stray wisp of hair back into her French twist. She smoothed down her skirt—the good navy-blue one she'd bought on sale last year—and turned to face her Aunt Bertha who was descending the stairs.

Aunt Bertha wasn't merely coming down the stairs. She was *descending*, floating along on a wave of White Shoulders perfume and yellowing lace and pink chiffon, Aunt Bertha's signature color. Sometimes Margaret Leigh got so tired of pink she wanted to scream. She never did, of course. Ladies didn't scream. They politely endured. And if there was one thing Margaret Leigh was, it was a lady.

She sighed. Sometimes she wished she had the courage to cuss. "I'll clean it up, Aunt Bertha. I'm sure Christine didn't mean to make a mess."

"She most assuredly did. That poodle peed on

the rug deliberately. She's been misbehaving ever since I came for my little visit."

Margaret Leigh rolled her eyes. Aunt Bertha's *little* visit. She'd come to Tupelo the previous April to find an apartment and to get away from the cold, damp weather in Chicago, where she'd been staying with Margaret Leigh's sister Tess. Now it was October, and Aunt Bertha was still in Margaret Leigh's house.

Of course, Margaret Leigh wouldn't dare complain. She'd been taught family loyalty, and family loyalty meant taking care of homeless maiden aunts, especially one who had practically raised her. Sometimes, though, she wished she had a little less loyalty and a little more backbone. Like Tess. Tess always said what she thought.

"Poodles are a nervous breed, Aunt Bertha. Christine will settle down in time."

Aunt Bertha was at the foot of the stairs now, panting and wheezing.

"Are you all right, Aunt Bertha?"

"Just let me catch my breath a minute." Bertha put a dimpled, bejeweled hand over her breast and sighed dramatically. "If I die tomorrow, all this will be yours, Margaret Leigh." She held out her hand so her fake diamonds would flash in the late-afternoon sun.

Margaret Leigh smothered a laugh. Aunt Bertha had been threatening to die for twenty years. Everybody in the family coddled her, pretending that both her diamonds and her aches and pains were real.

"Do you want to see a doctor, Aunt Bertha?"

"No, dear. I just need relief from that poodle of yours, and so I've made a few little arrangements."

"What arrangements?"

"I've engaged a dog trainer for Christine."

Margaret Leigh drew a big breath in anticipation of dealing with Aunt Bertha's latest effort at meddling. "That was . . . kind of you, Aunt Bertha, but I can't afford a dog trainer."

"Nonsense. A smart girl like you, making her way up the ladder of success at the library. You can't afford not to have a dog trainer. A woman bent on making something of herself can't have a dog that doesn't know how to behave in polite society."

"Number one, at thirty-two I'm hardly a girl. And number two, I'm not sure cataloguing books is making my way up the ladder of success. And even if it is, I can't see how making something of myself has anything to do with Christine's manners."

"She wets rugs, Margaret Leigh. And that's all there is to it. Now, I've already taken care of everything. You can take Christine tomorrow."

Margaret Leigh knew she'd been outmaneuvered, but she felt obliged to make at least a token protest. After all, she had her pride, even if it was always sitting on the backseat behind her manners.

"But tomorrow's Saturday. The trainer probably doesn't work on Saturday."

"I did some investigating. He hardly works at all unless he absolutely has to—not the kind of man I'd want any of my family consorting with under ordinary circumstances. But they say he's good. The best dog trainer in the county."

"I had planned to rake leaves tomorrow."

Aunt Bertha's face crumpled and both her chins trembled. "Of course, if you'd rather not . . ."

Stricken with guilt, Margaret Leigh patted her hand. "I'm sure you meant well. I suppose it won't hurt to talk to him."

"I just know he'll make a new woman of Christine."

The old Christine was all right with Margaret Leigh, but she didn't say so. Keeping the peace was what she did best. "You always have my best interests at heart, Aunt Bertha. I'll go tomorrow. After all, what can one little visit hurt?"

One

Andrew McGill loved Saturday mornings. He hung one long leg over the side of his hammock and pushed, setting the swing back into motion. Dry leaves crunched under his foot. Folding his hands behind his head, he listened to the music of autumn—wind soughing through the trees, quail calling to one another in the nearby fields, and his bird dogs baying in the backyard. The sky was so bright and shiny, it looked as if it had been scrubbed by industrious angels.

He sighed, content. Just give him an old pair of blue jeans, a few good bird dogs, and a lazy Saturday morning. What more could a man want?

The sun warmed his face, and he dozed for a while.

It was the barking that woke him up. Although his dogs had been baying when he'd gone to sleep, there was a new tremor in their voices, an edge of excitement that penetrated his sleep and brought him fully alert. Without getting up he swiveled his head and surveyed his surroundings.

Everything looked the same—the log cabin with

its blue chintz curtains, compliments of his sister Jo Beth; his old faithful Ford pickup, and his do-it-yourself flower bed, abloom with bronze chrysanthemums that made him think of football games and soggy hotdogs and bands playing too loud.

Then he saw the car. He couldn't believe his eyes. It was a yellow Volkswagen Beetle. He hadn't seen one of those in eighteen years. He shaded his eyes against the sun and watched the car rattle and bang its way down the dusty lane toward his cabin. The driver looker like a woman, but at a distance he couldn't tell.

He lay in his hammock, biding his time. He hadn't counted on company this Saturday morning, friends or otherwise, but he didn't mind the interruption. He would either send them scooting on their way so he could get back to his nap, or he would invite them to stay for a root beer.

The little car came to a sputtering halt beside his truck, and out stepped a tall woman. The next thing he noticed was the way she walked, regal, like a queen, but a bit stiff in the legs and back as if she weren't quite at ease. He grinned. She probably wasn't. His home was a shock to most women.

The woman paused in front of his cabin, eyeing it with the mortified look of a committee member on a mission of beautification. That was all he needed to ruin his Saturday morning—a do-gooder out to reform him. He closed his eyes and pretended to be asleep.

Margaret Leigh got over the shock of his cabin—it wasn't even painted, for goodness' sake—and plumped up her nerve enough to approach the man in the hammock. She tightened her hold on Christine, letting the familiar, warm body of the little dog give her courage.

The man was sprawled every which way, one arm flung backward over his head, one hanging off the side of the hammock, and his legs spread-eagled in total relaxation. He was tall and blond, and every inch of flesh showing was deeply tanned. She'd bet a penny he slept naked in the sun.

Her breath sucked in a little at the thought. Aunt Bertha had warned her about such men. Beer-drinking scoundrels who would never amount to a hill of beans. She would have thought the advice hopelessly old-fashioned if it hadn't proven to be true. The few Jones women who had had the misfortune of linking their fate with such a man had lived to rue the day. Her own sister was one of them.

As she stood watching the man, she felt a bead of sweat inch down the side of her face. A lone mosquito buzzed around her head, then finally settled on the man's right thigh. She watched in fascination as the mosquito marched across the tight jeans. A lump formed in her throat, and she discreetly cleared it.

"I don't bite except on Wednesdays."

Margaret Leigh jumped at the sound of the deep voice. Her gaze left the mosquito and flew to the man's face. It was crinkled with laughter.

"You startled me." She felt the heat of a flush on her cheeks.

"Are you real, or am I still asleep?" The man put his hands behind his head, hung one foot over the hammock and set the swing into motion again. Since she'd already ruined his nap, he decided he might as well have a little fun. "Only good girls blush. Are you a good girl?"

"Dear me." She fanned her face. "It's too hot for October."

"It's too hot for anything, even lovemaking."

"Goodness gracious." Margaret Leigh took a step backward. She could spot a scoundrel every time. They were interested in nothing except a woman's body.

Andrew McGill held back his chuckle. Keeping a serious face, he continued his outrageous behavior. "Have you ever made love in a hammock?" Her deepened color was his reward. "No, I guess not. You probably prefer cool white sheets and a four-poster. I'll bet you even wait until dark."

"My private life is none of your affair."

It was the first flash of spunk Andrew had seen. He was a bit relieved. He'd hate to be making mincemeat of a timid woman.

"The thing about making love after dark is that you have to do it mostly by feel. I prefer to see my lovers, don't you?"

The woman clutched her poodle closer to her chest and spun around. For a minute he thought she was going to leave. Then she whirled back, her cheeks rosy and her eyes blazing.

"If you would be so kind as to tell me how to find the dog trainer, I'll be happy to leave you to your lewd and lascivious remarks."

Andrew roared with laughter. The hammock rocked so hard with his mirth that when he sat up, he almost toppled out. "I've been called many things, but never lewd and lascivious."

"If the shoe fits, wear it."

"It pinches a little." Andrew stood up, but he didn't offer his hand. He was certain she wouldn't touch him, tarnished as he was. "Andrew McGill, at your service. Dog trainer extraordinaire."

"Good grief!"

"You could say that, too, I suppose, although most grief I've come across is not too good."

He was laughing again. Margaret Leigh had never seen a man who talked such foolishness and laughed while he was doing it. It only confirmed her first impression. He might be the county's best dog trainer, but he was first and foremost a scoundrel. Only her desire to keep the peace with Aunt Bertha made her stay.

"Aunt Bertha warned me that you were not the sort of man I'd want to consort with."

"Consort!" He laughed even harder. "Good Lord, woman, you call this consorting?" He reached out and ran his hand down the side of her flushed cheek. "I call *this* consorting." Her cheek felt so soft and downy, he decided to do it again. So he did.

She stepped back. "A gentleman would never touch a lady without her permission."

"I'm no gentlemen."

"You're a scoundrel."

"Most likely."

"And I wouldn't still be standing here if it weren't for Christine."

"Another moralistic aunt?"

"My dog."

Andrew looked over the quivering little animal in her arms. "Sorry. I don't train poodles."

"It's just as well. I wouldn't have wanted to leave her with you anyhow. She's nervous around strangers."

Andrew never could resist a challenge. He plucked the little poodle from her arms. With firm, sure strokes and soft, soothing words, he calmed Christine. When she licked his hand, Margaret Leigh was amazed.

"Animals are like women: they respond to a master's touch." Andrew winked at her.

"They said you were good with animals—"

"And women."

"—that's why I came to you."

"You did?"

She blushed again. "Because of Christine . . . and her problem."

He waited for her to elaborate. When she didn't, he prompted her. "You said Christine has a problem."

"It's her manners. She forgets them from time to time."

"She uses a spoon instead of a fork?"

"No. She . . ." Margaret Leigh paused. She'd never discussed things of an intimate nature with a man. She'd never even had a chance, what with nursing her sick father for six years and then taking care of whichever maiden aunt and down-on-her-luck cousin happened to come along. "She wets the rug, but only since my Aunt Bertha came to stay with us. Frankly, I think Christine is just a little jealous, and this is her way of vying for my attention. It's probably a passing thing, and she'll get over it in time."

She paused for breath, reaching for her dog all the while. At that moment, the thing she wanted most was to be out of Andrew McGill's presence. She'd never met such a disturbing man.

"If you'll hand Christine to me, I'll be on my way."

"Not so fast." Andrew continued stroking the little dog. "I've decided that training Christine will be a nice change of pace from training bird dogs."

"I don't want her to point, just to stop wetting the rug. I'll just take her and be on my way."

"You don't look like the scaredy-cat type to me."

"I'm not scared. I've changed my mind. That's all." She lied. She'd never been as scared in all her life. What was more, she didn't know which frightened her the most—that Andrew McGill would find her attractive or that he wouldn't.

"I'll tell you what: I'll make a deal with you. Leave Christine here for a few days, and if she's not minding her manners by next Saturday, you can take her home. No charge."

"And if she is?" Margaret Leigh hesitated. She'd always been uncomfortable discussing money. "You never did name your fee."

Andrew McGill considered the woman standing beside him. Whim had made him take on the poodle. He had no idea what prompted him to lower his fee. But he did just that, naming a fee that was so reasonable even the most avid bargain hunter would have been delighted.

Margaret Leigh hesitated only a moment. If Andrew McGill weren't careful, she'd be forced to revise her opinion of him.

"It's a deal." She held out her hand.

Andrew shook her hand solemnly. Then on another whim, he lifted it to his lips. He took his time with the kiss, lingering over her soft skin, inhaling its light floral fragrance. He could feel the heat of her blush all the way down to her fingertips.

Still holding her hand, he said, "You never did tell me your name."

"Margaret Leigh Jones." Her voice was breathless.

Andrew was pleased with himself as if he had won a National Field Trial trophy. Releasing her, he gazed into her eyes in the manner that he knew most women loved.

"Margaret Leigh Jones, your dog is in expert hands . . . and so are you."

"Mr. McGill—"

"Andrew."

"—I'm not in any man's hands." Margaret Leigh plucked up her courage enough to lean forward and tell her dog good-bye. "Christine, I'm going to leave you with this man for a day or two. But I'll be back. I promise you." She patted the little dog's head and accidentally brushed her hands against Andrew's. The hairs on her arms stood on end. She quickly withdrew her hand. "You'll be good to Christine, won't you?"

"Margaret . . ."

"Margaret Leigh."

He smiled. "Margaret Leigh, I might be a scoundrel through and through, but I know how to treat a dog. Trust me." He was surprised at himself. He never reassured the dog owners who came to him: he was a take-it-or-leave-it man. "If it will make you feel better, you can come back to visit her during the training."

"Thank you." She started to leave, then turned back for last-minute instructions. "She's afraid of the dark. I keep a night-light on for her. And she's vain. She loves to sleep in her ribbons. Loud noises bother her, so don't play the television too loud."

"I don't own a television."

"How do you keep up with current events?"

"Radio and newspapers."

"Well, keep the radio down low for Christine . . . please."

"Don't worry. She'll be returned to you safe and sound, but without her bad habit."

"Thank you." Margaret Leigh realized that was the second time she had said *thank you*. He must think she was a ninny. How did you deal with a man like Andrew McGill? Tess would know. She'd had experience. Margaret Leigh decided the best thing to do was just turn around and leave before she made any more blunders. With a little wave of her hand, she started off.

Andrew watched her go. Her eyes were the color of grape lollipops. The thought popped into his conscious mind unexpectedly. He'd never met a woman with eyes that color.

Christine whimpered, and he stroked her. "Your mistress is about the most uptight woman I've ever met. Did you know that, Christine?" The little dog licked his hand. "I've never seen such a proper lady."

The small car chugged around the bend and disappeared in a puff of dust.

"What would happen," Andrew mused, "if I trained *both* of you?" He chuckled at the thought. Teaching Margaret Leigh how to have fun might be just the thing to add some spice to his Saturday mornings. He'd think about it.

As soon as Margaret Leigh was around the bend, she pulled off the road and leaned her forehead on the steering wheel. She couldn't believe herself. She'd actually carried on with that man like a brazen hussy—letting him rub her cheek and calling him a scoundrel. What in the world had gotten into her? She should have taken her dog and marched right out of there. And that was another thing. She'd actually left Christine with the rogue. Of course, he *was* a dog trainer.

She took a handkerchief out of her purse and carefully wiped her perspiring palms. Southern ladies didn't sweat. Aunt Bertha had always told her that. So had Aunt Grace. Southern ladies didn't smoke standing up, either. She and Tess used to laugh over that bit of maidenly aunt wisdom. They'd get behind the barn with a pack of cigarettes Tess had swiped from Grandpa Jones and smoke standing up just to see if it made them feel like floozies. It never had. Of course Tess had gone on to become the family floozy—three divorces and singing in juke joints. At least, that was the family's opinion. It made Margaret Leigh as mad as . . . well, nearly as mad as hell.

She drew a deep breath. There. She'd thought it. "Hell." She even said it out loud. And it felt good.

If she had had a cigarette, she'd have climbed out of her car and smoked it standing up just for the heck of it. Maybe she was turning into a floozy. The strange thing was, it didn't feel bad, not bad at all.

She cranked her car and headed home. She knew her bold and reckless feelings were only temporary. Shy all her life and content to live in Tess's shadow, she was something of an anachronism, a woman with Victorian manners and morals in an age of easy sex and instant gratification.

Driving away from Andrew McGill's cabin, she wished she were different. She wished she wore bleached hair and leather skirts instead of a French twist and sensible gabardine. She wished she knew the art of banal banter and sexual innuendo rather than how to make Southern fried chicken and how to get dog piddle out of the rug. She wished she knew how to flirt instead of how to blush. She wished she preferred French kissing to French cooking.

Of course, she didn't wish any of that as a permanent condition, just on a short-term basis, just long enough to deal with the likes of Andrew McGill. She sighed. Maybe she'd feel more like herself after she raked the leaves.

Two

Andrew watched Margaret Leigh drive away until the last puff of dust had settled behind her car. Then he looked at the small dog in his arms.

"Now, what in the devil have I done?" His impulses were always getting him into trouble.

Christine whimpered. He patted her head.

"Don't mind me, sweetheart. It's not that I don't like you. I do. I love all animals, even ones that wet the rug."

Andrew chuckled, remembering Margaret Leigh's earnest expression when she tried to explain her dog's problem. Maybe it was her face, rosy with embarrassment, that had made him take on a poodle right when he was in the middle of Mississippi Rex's intensive training. There were only five months until the National Field Trial Championships. He couldn't afford to lose even one week of training. Heck, how was he going to train his bird dog to hold point with a nervous poodle looking on?

From his backyard came the sounds of his dogs howling.

"Hear that, Christine? They know somebody new is on the premises. Let's go back there and get you acquainted before they decide to take matters into their own hands."

Christine didn't like the bird dogs, and they didn't like her. Andrew had known that would happen. But he'd given his word, and he never backed down on his word. He'd just have to be patient, that was all.

He decided to take Christine inside and get her accustomed to her temporary home. The dogs bayed their displeasure at his leaving.

"Quiet down, old boys. This is Christine's day."

The back screen door popped behind him, and the poodle shivered. "She doesn't like loud noises." That's what Margaret Leigh had said in that earnest way she had of talking.

"Sorry about that, Christine." He set her on the kitchen floor and turned on the radio, keeping the volume low. "What is your pleasure in music? Pop? Classical? Country and Western?" He turned the dial as he talked, listening briefly to the offerings of the local radio stations. "No? My feelings exactly." He switched to an oldies channel, smiling as the relaxed strains of Glenn Miller's orchestra filled the room.

Christine squatted down next to him.

"No, you don't, young lady."

He got her outside just in time.

By afternoon, he and Christine had reached an uneasy truce; she gave up squatting in return for scratches behind the ear, exorbitant praise, and small doggie treats. If he had been the impatient kind, he'd have run out of patience about the same time he ran out of doggie treats. But

Andrew McGill was as relaxed and comfortable as an old chamois shirt after too many washings.

Stretched on his hammock with Christine resting across his stomach chewing her latest doggie treat, he watched two squirrels chase each other through the branches above his head. Nature was an endless delight to him.

"Look at that lady squirrel up there, Christine." Andrew scratched under the dog's fluffy chin. "She's a little con artist, pretending she's not interested when all the while she's dying to be romanced by that cocky old Don Juan. I've known lots of women like that. Playing hard to get, leading me a merry chase. Con artists, every one of them." He chuckled. "And I love them all."

Christine flopped her manicured tail and shook her pink hair ribbons as if to say, "Any fool can see that."

"Of course, every now and then I like a little variety. Take your mistress, for instance. I'll bet she's never tried to con a man in her life. Heck, I'll bet she's never even flirted with a man."

The idea intrigued him, and the more he thought about it the more intrigued he became. He thought about the way she had blushed and called him a scoundrel. He thought about her unusual eyes and the softness of her skin.

All the women he'd chased lately were alike—bright, witty, sophisticated, lovely to look at and lovely to touch. But they all wanted the same thing: they wanted Andrew to show them a good time, to take away the pressures of the hard-scrabbling, competitive lives they'd mapped out for themselves. They weren't like Margaret Leigh Jones. Not at all like Margaret Leigh with her old-fashioned manners and her old-fashioned virtues.

Another idea took hold. Variety. That's what he

wanted. He left the hammock and tucked Christine into a small towel-lined wicker basket on his kitchen floor.

"Take a nap, little girl. I'm going courting."

Margaret Leigh raked and hummed, while Aunt Bertha sat on the front porch knitting and watching and occasionally commenting.

"Margaret Leigh, you missed a spot, honey."

"Don't worry. I'll get to it."

Bird song and soft humming and the *clack* of knitting needles punctuated the long October silence. Then the needles stilled.

"Margaret Leigh, did you know that little Crocker girl?"

"Yes, Aunt Bertha. But she's hardly a girl. She's twenty-five or so, if I remember correctly."

"Well, she's in the family way. And her not even married. It'a a sin and a disgrace."

Margaret Leigh gave the leaves a good whack. Sometimes her aunt's outmoded ideas grated on her nerves, but she was immediately contrite for thinking even one bad thought about her family. She loved them, eccentric though they were.

"We shouldn't listen to idle gossip," she called over her shoulder. "And anyway, it's none of our affair."

"Well, still and all . . ."

Aunt Bertha fell into silence and Margaret Leigh hummed and raked. A while later, the knitting was shoved aside once more.

"Your hair is coming loose, honey. Maybe you ought to come inside and tuck it up."

"I'm almost finished, Aunt Bertha." Margaret Leigh leaned against her rake and tried to tuck her hair back into its pins, but the task was impossible. Her hair was heavy, and the autumn breezes plus the exertion of her work had caused it to slip its bonds. Finally she gave up and let it do what it wanted to do. Mouse hair, that's what it was. The dull, commonplace brown of an old mouse's coat. Tess's hair was glorious. The red gold of an October sunset. Margaret Leigh had always admired her sister's hair. But she had never envied her. Envy was as foreign to her as cussing.

She lifted her rake once more and dragged the fallen leaves to her ever-growing pile. She picked up her song again where she had left off, an old hymn, one of her favorites, "In the Sweet Bye and Bye." She was right in the middle of "We will meet on that beautiful shore," when she heard the truck coming. It was noisy and old, backfiring as it started up at the red light down the street.

Looking up, she shaded her eyes. She knew the truck. She'd seen it just that morning, a rakish, impossibly red Ford pickup truck sitting in the yard of none other than Andrew McGill. She tidied her hair and her face with one hand. Not that he was coming to see her, for goodness' sake. Why on earth would a man like that be coming to her house on a bright and sunny Saturday afternoon, when Tupelo was full of gorgeous, sophisticated women who probably knew how to French kiss and worse?

The noise grew louder as the truck came down Allen Street. And wonders of wonders, it stopped at the curb right in front of her house. Andrew McGill stepped out, as big as life and twice as jaunty.

"Margaret Leigh, that man is coming to our house!" Aunt Bertha exclaimed.

Margaret Leigh couldn't say a word. All she could do was cling to her rake and stare.

"Good Lord, Margaret Leigh. He's wearing a leather jacket. Only hoodlums wear leather jackets."

Andrew McGill heard that remark. Margaret Leigh could tell by the way he grinned. He enjoyed it too. Gracious, what a man!

He came across the yard, not stopping until he was so close she could see right through his blue eyes. She knew how Alice must have felt when she'd tumbled through the looking glass.

"Hello, Margaret Leigh." His voice was a rich baritone, deep and very formal. He was smiling like the devil come to claim a lost sinner. "Don't you look fetching with your hair falling loose?" He reached out and caught a strand of her hair between two fingers. "It looks like polished mahogany."

"Oh." It was all she could say. To make matters worse, she blushed again. She could feel the heat in the roots of her hair.

He tucked the strand of hair behind her ear and crammed his hands into his pockets, though the Lord only knew how he got them in there, tight as his jeans were. How did such a big man get into such a small pair of pants?

He chuckled. She'd been caught staring. One hand tightened on the rake and the other flew to her face.

"How—" Her voice came out a croak. She cleared her throat and started over. "How's Christine?"

"Like any woman who gets her way. Content."

"Margaret Leigh." At the sound of her aunt's voice, Margaret Leigh turned toward the front porch. She had completely forgotten about Aunt Bertha. "Who is that man?"

"The dog trainer, Aunt Bertha."

"Goodness gracious!"

That's what Margaret Leigh thought too. Goodness gracious. Andrew McGill turned toward the porch, all golden skinned and mannerly.

"Hello, there. I feel as if I know you already, Aunt Bertha." His manners were as smooth as molasses pouring from a jar. Before anybody knew what had happened, he was on the front porch, bending over Aunt Bertha's hand like some star out of a forties' movie. His lips barely brushed her skin. Then he smiled. "How charming you look in pink. It makes your skin just as pretty as magnolia blossoms."

"Well, I do declare." Aunt Bertha fluttered her eyes and flashed her fake diamonds.

Margaret Leigh propped her rake against a tree and joined them, selecting a straight-backed chair with a good view of her unexpected company.

"Won't you sit down?" she said to him. "Aunt Bertha, this is Andrew McGill. He's come to tell us about Christine."

"How sweet."

Andrew straddled a chair and grinned at them. "Actually, I've come courting."

The hiss of Aunt Bertha's breath was loud on the front porch. Margaret Leigh sat very still. She didn't know what to do or to say. It wasn't that she'd never had offers. Over the years, she'd had a few. But never from anyone as bold and reckless as Andrew McGill.

"I have dancing on my mind. . . . Do you dance, Margaret Leigh?"

"Well . . ." She wasn't about to admit that she hadn't danced since the high-school prom. "Everybody does some time or other."

"Good. There's a great place down Highway 45.

The root beer is cold, the band is better than most, and the owner doesn't cotton to fighting. What do you say we shake a leg around eight o'clock tonight?"

Margaret Leigh glanced from Aunt Bertha's pursed lips to Andrew McGill's wicked smile. "I have some professional reading I need to do tonight."

Aunt Bertha relaxed a little.

"I'll bet I'm more interesting than anything in your library." Andrew leaned closer and winked.

Margaret Leigh would bet the same thing. Temptation took a strong hold, and she almost yielded. Almost, but not quite.

"Mr. McGill, your offer is kind, but—"

"Kind? *Kind?*" He began to chuckle, and then the chuckle became a roar of full-bodied laughter.

"What's so funny about that?" Margaret Leigh was close to being miffed.

"I didn't invite you out of kindness. My motives are far less pure. And a lot more fun."

Andrew gave her a smile of such persuasive radiance that she felt like melting into a little puddle at his feet. She rallied her resistance for one more protest.

"Your motives are probably most improper."

"If you call an urge to dance improper, they are." His smile gathered force, picking up radiance until he was positively gleaming.

She yielded a little. "Of course, the weather is gorgeous, and it's going to be such a nice night for dancing."

Beside her, Aunt Bertha sounded like a fat party balloon that had just lost its air. Andrew kept gleaming at her. That's the best word she could use to describe him. It wasn't merely his smile: it was his teeth and his skin and his hair.

He gleamed all over. And *oh*! he was hard to resist. She took a deep breath and talked very fast, before she could change her mind.

"I guess I could do that reading later. Yes, I'll go with you."

"Margaret Leigh, I'm going to show you the time of your life." Andrew stood up, all grace and charm and ease. "Be ready at eight, pretty one." He turned smoothly to Aunt Bertha and took her hand once more. "Don't worry about your niece. I plan to take good care of her."

The two women sat on the front porch, stunned, while he took his leave. His jaunty whistle echoed across the yard as he sauntered toward his pickup truck. The old door creaked when he opened it. With one foot on the floorboard he saluted. Then he rattled and banged down Allen Street and out of sight.

Aunt Bertha found her tongue first. "What in the world came over you, Margaret Leigh?"

"An urge to dance, Aunt Bertha."

"But with a man like that. Did you see all that skin he had showing above his shirt? It's not decent."

"Golden and gorgeous is what I would call it."

"Margaret Leigh!"

Margaret Leigh stared dreamily into the distance. What *had* come over her? She didn't know, and she didn't want to question. All she wanted to do was go dancing with Andrew McGill.

"Did you notice? He called me pretty one?"

"And it took the brains right out of your head. Now don't look at me with those big wounded eyes. Honey"—Aunt Bertha reached for her hand—"a man like that . . ." She patted and stared into the distance. "A nice girl like you has to be careful."

"I've been careful all my life."

"Still and all . . ."

"It's not that I'm going to go out and turn wild. I've been good all my life, and I can't see any reason to change that. But Aunt Bertha . . . I'm missing something by only going out with dull men."

"Nice men. *Safe* men."

"Dull. Dull as dishwater."

Aunt Bertha opened her mouth once or twice, but no sound came out. She struggled with her conscience a long while, then she gave Margaret Leigh's hand a final pat. "Promise me you'll be careful, honey. I'd die if anything bad happened to you."

"I'll be careful. And anyhow, Aunt Bertha, what could possibly happen on a dance floor?"

By the time eight o'clock came and she was sitting on her side of Andrew's pickup truck, feeling scared and hugging the door handle, she decided that more than she bargained for might happen on a dance floor. More than she'd bargained for was happening to her right there sitting in a pickup truck.

For one thing, Andrew McGill looked delicious in the dark. With the streetlights shining through the windows, he looked as polished as a gold saint. But there was nothing saintly about his smile, or his voice, or his conversation. Gracious, it was enough to make her quiver.

She kept her hands tightly clasped so he wouldn't notice. She'd be darned if she'd quiver like some unused little shrinking violet. Even if that's what she was.

"You look mighty pretty in that party dress, Margaret Leigh. All bright and shiny like a brand new Christmas ornament." He flashed his winning smile at her. "I love Christmas." He reached across the seat and caressed the shimmery blue material over her thigh. "Nice. What's that fabric called?"

"Taffeta."

"You'll have to speak up, pretty one. I'm used to bird dogs baying all the time. I guess my hearing's going bad."

"Taffeta!"

"Taffeta. It has a nice ring. Like something good to eat."

They stopped at a traffic light, and mercifully his rusty old brakes covered the sound of her nervous breathing. She made herself do a slow count to ten and settle into a normal breathing pattern. Just think of him as another Harry Cox, she told herself, the safest, dullest man in all of Tupelo. He never even held her hand without permission.

"Why don't you scoot a little closer?"

She jerked out of her semitrance. "I beg your pardon?"

"Scoot a little closer, Margaret Leigh."

"I'm comfortable, thank you."

"For me?" He gave her a heart-tugging smile. "My reputation is going to be ruined if folks see me going down the street with enough room to put a kindergarten class between me and my date." He looked so innocent, she gave in and inched a little closer.

"That's better." He slid his arm along the back of the seat and draped it over her shoulders. She'd never known that a man's arm could feel so alive, as if it were plugged into an electrical socket. "Don't you think that's better?"

"Well . . . it's closer."

Andrew laughed. It was a big, hearty sound

that seemed to make the whole truck vibrate. "You're a treat, Margaret Leigh. With those big purple eyes and that soft shiny hair and that pretty shy smile, I don't know why some man hasn't snatched you off the streets long before this. Why is that?"

"Some men don't appreciate the serious type."

She was beginning to feel a little better. She hadn't done anything to disgrace herself. Not yet, anyhow. She certainly had the intelligence to carry on a conversation. She was even discovering the freedom to speak her mind. And it felt wonderful.

"Are you the serious type?" he asked.

"I've never really thought about what type I am. Have you?"

"I guess I'm a lewd and lascivious scoundrel."

"I probably shouldn't have said those things. That was very ungracious of me."

"I enjoyed it."

"You did? Why?"

"I've discovered that few people speak their minds. Most of them play word games, saying only what they think a person wants to hear. It's refreshing to hear the truth."

"My. You are a puzzle, Andrew McGill."

He turned toward her, and in the flash of the streetlights she saw a serious expression on his face. "Solve me."

He had to be kidding, of course. Why would a man like Andrew want a woman like her to delve deep enough to know the mysteries of his mind, the complexities of his spirit?

"Is that a new line? A nineties-decade way for men to keep a woman interested?"

He roared with laughter. "By George, Margaret Leigh, you have spunk."

"On occasion." She smiled at him. She was beginning to enjoy her date.

"I'll see what I can do to make those occasions happen more frequently."

"Why?"

"You're a pretty woman."

"I'm not all that pretty. And I'm certainly not stupid. I'm not dumb enough to believe that a worldly man like you has more than a passing curiosity for a woman like me."

"Curiosity leads to great discoveries. . . . Columbus exploring America."

"I'm not a new continent. And I'm not about to be explored."

He laughed so hard, he almost rear-ended the car in front of them. When he'd finished laughing, he turned to her. "If you'll scoot just a little closer, I promise that I won't try to explore you. At least, not yet."

"Why do you want me to sit closer? I've already scooted over once."

"Because we'll be at the Pirates' Den in about five minutes, and if I know Hooter and James Johnson, they'll be out in the parking lot, sitting on the tailgate of Hooter's truck, watching to see who's coming to the Saturday-night dance."

"And your reputation will be ruined if they see enough room to stuff a balloon between us?"

"Right."

"Why do you care?"

"I don't care what other people say. I just like to brag. I like to say that all women find me irresistible."

She did. In the last fifteen minutes she'd found him totally irresistible, and she couldn't have said why any more than she could have flown to the moon without wings.

She was already close enough to feel his body heat, but what was the harm in moving closer? His arm tightened at the same time she made some slight movement. She found herself thigh to thigh with him, pressed tightly as a skin on summer sausage. Her heart thumped hard against her ribcage, and she imagined that he heard.

"Look over yonder." As he pulled into the Pirates' Den, he nodded toward a sleek black Chevrolet truck. "Perched like two jaybirds on a limb. Hooter and James, the town's bad boys . . . except for me."

Her heart did a quick fandango. She'd suspected it, and now he'd confirmed it. She was on a date with Tupelo's bad boy. Margaret Leigh Jones, the most inexperienced woman this side of the Mississippi, was set to enter the Pirate's Den with a man she couldn't handle if she had a whip and a chair. She lifted her chin in a small gesture of determination. She'd just have to keep her wits about her, that was all.

"Well, looka here!" The voice echoed across the parking lot as she and Andrew got out of the truck.

"Hooter," Andrew whispered in her ear.

"Looka what Andrew's got. Where'd you get that beauty, boy?"

"I don't tell trade secrets, Hooter."

"It's ain't right not to share, Andy." The gruff voice belonged to James.

"Look but don't touch, boys."

Keeping his arm around her, Andrew quickly drew her into the nightclub. The encounter in the parking lot was nothing compared to the shock of entering the Pirates' Den. Smoke fogged the room, circling the naked bulbs like blue vultures. Skin was showing everywhere. Women with naked shoulders and skirts hiked up to show their mesh-stockinged legs were sitting at tiny tables with men wearing cowboy hats and snakeskin boots and smoking big, ugly cigars. The loud music and loud voices combined in a roar that filled the club. There was a small parquet dance floor, but it was so crowded, a toothpick wouldn't have fit between the dancers.

"Do you like it?" Andrew had to yell in her ear to be heard.

"It's . . . different."

"From what, pretty one?"

"From professional reading."

Laughing, he wove his way through the crowd, keeping her safely tucked against him. By some miracle, he found a table about the size of six large postage stamps in a far corner of the room. She slid into a chair, bumping two people on her descent.

"Excuse me," she said. They didn't even look her way.

"It happens all the time." Andrew sat across from her. His legs got all tangled up with hers. She tried to move away, but there was nowhere to move. So she sat at the crowded table with her knees between Andrew's and her thighs pressing against his as if she were some shady lady of the evening. She supposed it was indecent, but it didn't feel that way. It felt slightly naughty and almost comfortable and ever so exhilarating.

Andrew reached across the table and linked his hands with hers. "How about a good tall glass of root beer to cool things off."

"Root beer?"

"You don't like it?" He looked crestfallen, as if she'd just said she didn't like his grandmother.

"Yes, I like it. It's just that I never imagined a

man like you drinking root beer instead of Old Crow."

"You keep saying 'a man like you,' as if I'm from some other planet. I'm just an ordinary bird-dog trainer, living in the woods and getting my kicks by dancing with pretty women on Saturday nights."

"You're far from ordinary, Andrew McGill."

"Tell me more." He leaned so close, she had the sensation of falling into his eyes for the second time that day. "Like all human beings, I love to hear good things about myself." He squeezed her hand. "You will say good things, won't you, Margaret Leigh?"

"If you call bold to the point of swaggering good, I suppose I will."

"Swagger. I like that term. Do I swagger?" He was as pleased as a little boy by the prospect.

"You could out-swagger Bluebeard the Pirate."

"You have quite a turn with words."

"I suppose that's because I read all the time."

"A pretty woman like you . . . with that soft pearly skin." He ran the back of his hand lightly down her cheek. "You should be making love all the time."

"I . . ." She wet her dry lips with the tip of her tongue. *Think. Change the subject.* "Actually, I should be good with words. I'm surrounded by books."

"Where?"

"In the library. I'm the cataloguer."

"A librarian."

"You make me sound like a museum piece."

"No. I think it's great." He traced her cheek again. "A lovely librarian in a shiny Christmas dress . . . and you're all mine."

She forced herself to hold her head up. My, how

he made a girl go limp. "Actually, I'm not all yours. I'm a woman of independent means making something of myself and living a quiet, decent life on Allen Street with a poodle named Christine and an aunt named Bertha."

As always, his laughter came quickly. Margaret Leigh liked that about him, his quick laughter. She liked it almost as much as she did his extraordinary blue eyes.

"Woman of independent means, may I have this dance?" The band was playing a slow bluesy tune.

"Yes."

He maneuvered his big body out of the small space behind the table and scooted out her chair, in the manner of a real gentleman. She put her hand in his, and he led her to the dance floor. Sliding one arm around her shoulders, Andrew squeezed them into an opening about the size of a rake handle.

Every inch of her was pressed against him from chest to knee. He was as solid as an oak tree and as inviting as a warm fire on a cold day. And rhythm! Although she hadn't danced in many years, she had no trouble following Andrew's lead.

This was the way it should be, she thought. A man and a woman moving in close embrace and perfect harmony, surrounded by dim smoky lights and sweet blues. For the first time in all her thirty-two years, she felt sad for all the things she'd missed—the Saturday-night dances, the sunshine and pine needles smell of a man's skin, the rough-soft feel of his cheek against hers, the heart-thumping thrill of his hand low on her back.

"You were born to be held, Maggy."

Nobody ever said things like that to her. And nobody ever called her Maggy except Tess, bold

Tess, who could do and say anything and still make people love her.

Since she could think of no suitable reply, Margaret Leigh said nothing. He pulled her so close, she was almost in his pocket. How they could dance that way was beyond her. She didn't care. What they were doing in the small space wasn't really dancing anyhow. It was more like making love standing up. At least, she supposed that's what it was like. Tess had told her. And of course she'd read her share of books and seen her share of television and movies. Nothing much was left to the imagination anymore. All the mystery was gone.

Except for Margaret Leigh. For her, there was still the mystery of the unknown. And the glory. What would it feel like? What would it sound like? Smell like?

Curiosity leads to great discoveries. She heard Andrew's voice as clearly as if he had spoken. Land sakes, what had gotten into her? Curiosity also lead to things like hasty marriages and nasty divorce and bitter feelings. If she had forgotten that, all she had to do was pick up the telephone and call Tess. Tess would tell her.

She'd do well to stick to her dancing and forget about exploring the male continent.

Three

Andrew was having a good time.

That didn't come as any surprise to him. He always managed to have a good time. What surprised him was that he liked Margaret Leigh Jones, really *liked* her. She was soft and sweet-smelling and feminine in addition to being quick witted. He liked a woman with wit.

By George, sometimes his impulses paid off. If he hadn't taken on that spoiled poodle, he wouldn't be at the Pirates' Den with Margaret Leigh. Life was just full of unexpected pleasures.

"Put your head on my shoulder, pretty one." He cupped the back of her head, enjoying the feel of her silky hair, and settled her against his shoulder. She was a little stiff and uncomfortable, but she fit very well.

"You know what I love about this place?" He had to lean close and speak directly in her ear so she could hear him. It gave him the advantage of feeling her soft hair against his cheek and smelling her fragrance.

"No. Tell me."

She twisted slightly, and he found his mouth only inches from hers. Funny, he had never noticed her mouth before. It was full and beautifully defined. Lush. The prim librarian had a lush mouth. Her body felt good too. He ran his hand experimentally down her back, enjoying the feel of her blue taffeta dress and the shiver that went through her.

When he'd seen her in that dress, he'd felt some long-lost innocence bubble up inside him. He hadn't seen a girl put on a party dress to go dancing since his college days. Nowadays, they opted for comfort, mostly old blue jeans and baggy sweaters and sneakers. But Margaret Leigh had worn blue taffeta for him. Somehow that made him feel good.

He leaned a fraction closer so that his lips were almost touching hers. "What I like, Margaret Leigh, is being in the middle of a crowd and feeling entirely alone. It's a strange kind of privacy."

Her eyes widened, and a soft flush came into her cheeks. She's afraid I'm going to kiss her, he thought. He would have if she had been any other woman. But she was Margaret Leigh Jones, wearing a dress of blue taffeta and a cloak of innocence. And so he decided to wait. He had all the time in the world. He wasn't out for a conquest. He was just after a little variety.

"Sometimes you say the most wonderful things," she said.

"That's wonderful?"

"Yes." Her smile was shy and beautiful. "Comparing my dress to Christmas . . . that's poetic."

"Thank you."

"You could have laughed, you know."

"Why?"

She glanced down at his jeans, T-shirt, and

leather jacket. "It appears that I'm terribly over-dressed."

"I figure a man is never overdressed if he's comfortable. Are you comfortable?"

"Well . . ." She bit her lower lip. "This dress puts me in a party mood. It makes me feel sparkly and sort of young. So yes, I guess you could say I'm comfortable."

"Then relax a little more. I don't bite." He pressed her head against his shoulder once more. "Here. Let me massage your back. Is that better?"

"Yes."

He knew she was lying. She was stiff all the way down to her toes. And that made him feel like a king as well as a scoundrel. He'd have to spend all day tomorrow walking in the woods and trying to figure that out. He wasn't accustomed to ambiguities in his life. Simplicity was more his style.

He kept her on the dance floor for nearly an hour. The band was in a mellow mood and played nothing but slow jazzy tunes that were nice for cuddling. And there was nothing he enjoyed more than cuddling, unless it was lying in the sunshine listening to his dogs bay.

When they finally sat down, Margaret Leigh was dewy-faced and wide-eyed. Looking at her through the haze of blue smoke, Andrew felt invigorated.

"How about that root beer now?"

"Sounds good."

"I'll go and get it. Stay right here."

"Where would I go?"

He kept an eye on her as he edged through the crowd toward the bar. When he was halfway across the room, he saw Hooter making his way toward Margaret Leigh. He was torn between going back to the table and going on to the bar. Finally he decided to go for the root beer. Margaret Leigh was a grown woman. He didn't want to insult her by acting as if he thought she didn't have enough gumption to take care of herself.

He leaned across the bar, ordered quickly, then turned around so he could see what Hooter was doing. As far as Andrew knew, he was harmless, but he did have a way of leering that scared the wits out of some women.

Hooter was standing close to Margaret Leigh, too darned close for Andrew's liking—and he was laughing his head off. He'd probably made some fool joke that he thought was funny. Or perhaps Margaret Leigh had said something witty. Hooter leaned over and cut off Andrew's view of their table.

For the first time in his life he felt impatient. "Is that root beer about ready?"

"Coming right up."

He slapped the money on the bar, then quickly took the frosty glasses across the room, sloshing some of the amber liquid onto the wooden bar. Margaret Leigh was sitting serenely at their table with her hands folded, and Hooter was in full retreat.

"You had company while I was gone." Andrew plopped the glasses on the table.

"Yes. Mr. Hooter."

"Mister!" Andrew laughed. "He must have loved that."

"He hated it." She took a sip of her root beer, made only a small face, then took another sip.

"Well . . ." Andrew left the word hanging.

"Well, what?"

"Aren't you going to tell me what Hooter wanted?"

"To dance."

"That's all he wanted, to dance? Then why did he leave in such a hurry?"

"I suppose it's because I told him I'm a one-man woman, and you'd already put your mark on me and there was no telling what you'd do if I strayed." She gave him a guileless look. "Do you think lying's a sin, Andrew?"

He took a long while answering. A flip answer might have been suitable for a teasing question, but Margaret Leigh's question had been completely artless. He'd bet on that. "I think it depends on the circumstances. It seems to me that at times a well-meaning lie is kinder than the truth."

She smiled. "I believe you're a nice man, Andrew McGill."

"Promise not to tell."

"I was thinking of putting it on little stickers and pasting them in all the library books."

They sipped their root beer and laughed and talked of inconsequential things and studied each other on the sly. He thought she was the most unusual woman he'd ever met, and she thought he was the most complex man she'd ever known. He marveled at her innocence, and she marveled at his boldness. He thought she'd really be beautiful if she'd let her hair down and loosen up and smile more often, and she thought he'd be a fine catch if he tried harder to make something of himself.

In the midst of a discussion about movies, he leaned forward and caught her hand. "Margaret Leigh, which part did you lie about? Your being a one-man woman or me putting my mark on you?"

"Both," she said. Neither, she thought.

"Good." He wasn't above telling a lie himself.

"Playing the field makes life more interesting, don't you think?"

"Definitely." She had no idea.

"I'm glad we think alike." He thought she lied with grace and charm.

The band struck up another slow tune, and Andrew escorted her to the dance floor once more. They surprised themselves at how much they liked dancing together. And midnight surprised them both.

When Margaret Leigh looked up at the big clock on the wall, glowing with red and blue neon, she couldn't believe it. "Gracious, it's getting late."

He glanced at his watch. "Midnight's the shank of the evening, but it did come fast."

"I have to go home."

"I can promise you my pickup doesn't turn into a pumpkin."

"I don't like to leave Aunt Bertha alone too long. She's old and she does have a few health problems."

It was the first time he'd ever left the Pirates' Den before two o'clock. Hooter and James yelled something he didn't hear when he passed their way. It was just as well. What they had said wasn't fit for a lady's ears anyhow.

He helped Margaret Leigh into his truck, got behind the wheel, and headed back to Allen Street. He'd thought she would be more relaxed going home than she had been coming, but she wasn't. It didn't take him long to figure out why. She expected him to make his move.

He whistled a tune under his breath and thought about his move. He wanted to kiss her. That much was definite. He'd been wanting to ever since he noticed her lush lips. He surprised himself by discovering he wanted more, too. Holding her close had been a powerful aphrodisiac. Move with caution, he warned himself. She's unschooled in the ways of courtship and love.

He parked his truck in the shadow of an old oak tree and walked her to her door, one hand resting lightly on the small of her back. He felt a tremor run through her when they mounted the steps. It heightened his anticipation. He could almost feel her lips under his, hesitant and shy at first, then open and hungry as he stoked the fires he knew were there.

At the front door, he turned her lightly in his arms. The porch light caught the brightness in her red-brown hair and the fear in her eyes.

He'd expected nervousness, but not fear. It took him aback.

"Well," she said. "Thank you for a lovely evening."

She bit her trembling lower lip, and he knew he couldn't do it, at least not the way he had planned.

"Thank *you*, Margaret Leigh." He retreated a step feeling noble and self-sacrificing as he bent over her hand. Brushing his lips across her palm, he caught the scent of her skin. It was an old-fashioned fragrance, a mixture of roses and the lilacs he remembered growing around the gazebo at his grandmother's house. He lingered a while longer, then straightened and released her.

"It was my pleasure to have the prettiest girl at the Saturday-night dance."

"You're teasing."

"No. I'm bragging." He gave a crooked grin and a smart salute. "We'll dance again. Good night, pretty one."

He left her porch and went down her sidewalk, whistling. He was inordinately proud of himself. He felt like a missionary on an errand of mercy. Or a scientist working on a secret formula. Or Pygmalion bringing a statue to life. But Margaret Leigh was no stone statue. She was flesh and blood and roses and lilacs. She was china skin and shy glances. She was a project. *His* project.

He climbed into his truck and headed home to his dogs.

Margaret Leigh let herself quietly inside and leaned against the door. Outside she could hear the engine sputtering and backfiring. She put her hand over her heart. She knew just how that old engine felt. She was sputtering and backfiring herself. She had been scared . . . and he'd known it.

He must think she was the silliest woman who ever drew breath. Lord, what a mess. She closed her eyes. But that didn't help a bit. She still saw Andrew, big and handsome and virile, and looking at her as if he planned to eat her for breakfast. He probably had all the women he wanted for breakfast. Why in the devil did she think he wanted to add her to his diet?

Experience. There had been one time back in college when she'd decided to experiment, to defy her upbringing, to ignore all Aunt Bertha's dire warnings and find out for herself. It had been Halloween, an evening as crisp and clear as polished red apples. Her date had been tall and good-looking, a blind date arranged by Barb, the dorm's most popular girl.

It hadn't taken him long to maneuver her away from the party and into his car. He'd mentioned the bluff, and she'd nodded, knowing what was coming next, terrified but anxious to get it over with. He had been all hands, clumsy and sweaty and grasping. And in the end she had fought, using her elbows and her knees and her fingernails. Fortunately for both of them, her date had finally been too wise to press the matter. He'd brought her home with her stockings torn and her virtue intact.

She'd never tried to experiment again. Not that she had had the time. Her father, a life-long diabetic, had become an invalid her last year of graduate school. She'd cared for him until his death two years before, staying in the old family home, working at the library during the day and sitting with her father during the evenings. But she hadn't regretted it. Not much, at least. Not until tonight. At the thought of Andrew McGill's arms around her and his body pressed closed to hers, she was filled with longing, longing to be the kind of woman who kissed as naturally as she breathed, the kind of woman who encouraged a man's embrace and knew what to do once she was in his arms.

"Aunt Bertha," she whispered, "what have you done to me? Why?"

She pulled off her shoes and tiptoed up the stairs to her safe attic bedroom.

"Good morning, Aunt Bertha."

Bertha jumped and slammed her diary shut at the same time. "Lord, child, you scared me to death. What are you doing up so early?" Pushing her straggly hair back from her face, she looked up at Margaret Leigh standing in the doorway. Her color was higher than usual. A hard lump of fear settled in Bertha's stomach.

"It's not early, Aunt Bertha. It's almost time for

church." Margaret Leigh came into the room.
"You look peaked. Didn't you sleep well?"

"Actually, I didn't. I was too worried to sleep."

Margaret Leigh came into the downstairs bedroom, which had become Aunt Bertha's since her
advent, and sat on the edge of the bed.

"I hope you're not worried about a place to stay.
My home is yours for as long as you like."

"I don't like to keep imposing on you and Tess."

"It's not an imposition. You've been a mother
to us. We want to take care of you. You deserve
that."

"There are some in the family who would dis-
agree with you."

"Who?"

"Grace."

At the mention of her mother's younger sister,
Margaret Leigh wrinkled her nose. There had
been three Adams sisters—Bertha, the oldest
and, judging by old photographs, the prettiest;
Margaret, the only one who had married; and
Grace, the baby, with a build like a grizzly bear
and a temper to match. If fate had to decree the
death of the gentle Margaret Adams Jones, Margaret Leigh was thankful that at least Bertha and
not Grace had been left in charge. Aunt Bertha
had been strict, too strict Tess always said; but
Aunt Grace would have been impossible. She considered it her duty to tell the entire family what
to do. Aunt Bertha even remarked that if Grace
weren't so scared of hell fire and damnation, she'd
tell God how to run the world.

"Don't pay any attention to what Aunt Grace
says."

"She says I ought to get a little apartment of
my own and leave you girls to yourselves."

Margaret Leigh felt guilty that she had sometimes thought the same thing. She crossed the room and put her arms around her aunt's shoulders.

"Put that thought right out of your head. I'll take care of you." She smoothed her aunt's straggly gray hair back from her face. It was not like Aunt Bertha to neglect combing her hair. "I don't want you worrying another minute."

Bertha's eyes were watery when she looked up at Margaret Leigh. "That dog trainer. He didn't do anything to you, did he?"

Margaret Leigh squelched her irritation. If Aunt Bertha acted as if she and Tess were still sixteen instead of over thirty, it was only because she loved them. And she was getting old.

"We danced, Aunt Bertha. That's all."

"He seemed the wild type to me. Maybe you shouldn't see him again, honey."

"Don't worry, Aunt Bertha. I'm plenty old enough to take care of myself."

"Still and all . . ."

"Anyhow, chances are very good he'll never ask me for another date. I don't think I'm his type."

"Don't look so crestfallen over it, honey." Patting Margaret Leigh's hand, she added, "Someday the right man will come along, a real proper gentleman. Just you wait and see."

Margaret Leigh wanted to say if she waited much longer, she'd be too old to care, but she didn't. Instead she kissed the top of her aunt's head and went into the kitchen to prepare breakfast.

That Sunday Margaret Leigh did everything in her usual way. She went to church and afterward took her aunt to lunch. Then she went with her

Sunday-school class to Traceway Manor to visit the shut-ins. When she got home, she put a roast into the oven for supper and settled onto the sofa with the Sunday paper.

But she didn't feel usual at all. She kept having breathless moments, and every now and then her cheeks got hot. She knew what was the matter with her. Andrew McGill. He'd made her feel pretty. Even desirable. She was very close to being smitten.

She folded the paper in her lap and stared into space. What was he doing now? Was he thinking about the previous night? Was he remembering how it felt to stand so close on the dance floor, pressed up against her so he could hardly tell where one body left off and the other began?

"Don't be foolish, Margaret Leigh."

The sound of her own voice brought her back to her senses. What was she thinking of? Even if by some miracle he did ask her out again, what in the world would she ever do with a man like him? A man who lived in the woods with his bird dogs. Everybody on both sides of her family tried to make something of themselves. There was even a governor on her mother's side. It wouldn't do for her to fall in love with a vagabond like Andrew.

She opened her paper and turned to the arts section. She'd be better off if she quit mooning and stuck to book reviews. She was well into a review of Stephen King's latest when she realized that she wasn't going to spend the rest of the afternoon reading. For once in her life, she was going to be daring.

Almost in a trace, she laid the paper aside and went upstairs. She freshened her lipstick and turned to get her purse. On second thought, she took the pins from her French twist and brushed out her hair. It hung heavy and silky around her cheeks, and she felt young and giddy. Grabbing her coat and purse, she went downstairs.

Bertha was sitting beside the window in her bedroom, still wearing her Sunday hat. Margaret Leigh quickly crossed the room and slid an arm around her shoulders.

"Aunt Bertha, what in the world are you doing?"

"Watching the birds."

Margaret Leigh started to comment on the hat. Instead, she removed it and gently smoothed her aunt's hair.

"It's a nice afternoon for bird watching."

Aunt Bertha slowly turned from the window. The first thing she saw was Margaret Leigh's hair. The next thing she saw was the purse.

"Are you going somewhere, honey?"

For the first time in her life, Margaret Leigh lied to Aunt Bertha—to spare her any needless worry, she told herself. "Just on an errand. Will you watch the pot roast while I'm gone?"

"Certainly." Aunt Bertha caught her hand. "Be careful."

Margaret Leigh deliberately misunderstood the warning."

"I always drive carefully."

It was almost sunset by the time she got to Boguefala Bottom. She parked her car beside Andrew's red truck and mounted the cabin steps. Her knock was timid at first, and then bolder when she failed to rouse anybody. By the fourth knock she decided no one was home.

She turned and started back down the steps.

"Going somewhere?"

She whirled at the sound of his voice. Andrew

was standing in the doorway, chest bare, jeans snug over his hips, and a guitar dangling from his hands. She couldn't seem to take her eyes off his chest. Fascinated, she studied each muscle separately, as if they were rare museum pieces. The setting sun spotlighted him, tangling in his gold chest hairs, so that every inch of him shimmered.

"Would you like to take a bite, Margaret Leigh?"

Her head snapped up. "I beg your pardon?"

He crossed the porch, took her hand, and dragged her into his cabin. "I do love it when a woman looks at me like that." He pulled her inside and kicked the door shut behind them. "Yessir, there's nothing to liven up a good Sunday evening like a woman who wants to have me for supper."

Four

Andrew was delighted with the turn of events.

He'd spent all Sunday congratulating himself on moving with caution. He'd never set out to reform a woman before, but he guessed it was best done slowly. There she was, though, at his cabin in Bougefala Bottom with that certain look in her eyes that he knew so well; the look of a woman who wanted a man.

"Yessir. This is an unexpected pleasure. Have a seat, Margaret Leigh." He released her, and she made her way to a rocking chair. "No, not way over there. Sit over here on the couch by me. It's friendlier that way."

She caught the back of the rocking chair like a seasick sailor clinging to a lifeboat.

"I'm not here to be friendly." She took a deep, shuddering breath. "Or to have you for supper."

"A pity. You would have liked it."

"Is it this place that makes you so crude?" Color smudged her cheeks and anger brightened her eyes. "Last night you were a perfect gentleman. I almost thought there was hope for you."

"Hope for *me*." Andrew was astonished. He was all set to show her a good time, and she was acting as if he'd committed a felony. Maybe she was beyond his help. Right now she was cased in ice so thick, it would have taken a blowtorch to thaw her out. And he had just the torch. He deliberately positioned himself so she could get the best view of his chest. Then he baited the hook. "Why tinker with perfection, Margaret Leigh?"

"Who do you think you are, Andrew McGill? God's gift to women?"

"Yes." He deliberately goaded her.

"Well, you're not. You're just a . . . a . . ." She touched her hands to her hot cheeks, and finally sank into the rocking chair. "Dear me. All I did was come to see about my dog."

Andrew could have kicked himself. She wasn't a project. She was a human being, a shy, vulnerable woman who had apparently broken all her rigid rules in coming to his cabin. And he was acting the arrogant ass, treating her like an object.

He moved quickly, crossing the room and squatting beside her before she could bolt and run.

"I'm sorry, Margaret Leigh." He tipped her face up with one hand. "Look at me." With his other hand he smoothed her hair back. "You wore your hair down."

She nodded, never taking her eyes from his face.

"I like it like that."

"Thank you."

Always the proper lady. He felt a great well of protectiveness rise in him.

"You won't leave until I apologize, will you?"

"You've already done that." She smiled then, her lips curving shyly upward.

"No, I haven't. You came to see about your dog, and I assumed you were after my lithe, tan body."

"It *is* lithe and tan." Her gaze raked his chest, then she blushed.

"Thank you." Nobody had ever blushed at the sight of his chest. It made him feel good and noble. He sat back on his heels and smiled at her, out to prove that gallantry in the Southern male was not dead. He needed to redeem himself.

"I was sitting here playing my guitar with nothing but bird dogs for company, and then you walked in the door. For a minute I lost my head. It just went right out of my mind that you're a proper lady who would never come to a man's house for anything more than a neighborly visit."

Margaret Leigh suspected he was making all that up for her benefit. Her heart melted. Andrew McGill was a puzzle, a wickedly innocent man who maddened her and teased her and intrigued her as no man ever had. And he was taking all the blame for their misunderstanding on himself. She couldn't let him do that.

"Actually, I didn't just come to see Christine."

"You didn't?" His smile was her reward.

"I came to see you too. I even thought about asking you to a family dinner."

"Are you still thinking about it?"

"Off and on."

"During one of your on times, ask me."

"All right." She wished she had the courage to be bold, but she didn't. Instead she leaned back in her rocking chair, shifting her legs in order to break contact with him.

He took her movement as a signal and stood up. Going back to the couch, he picked up his guitar. "If you can stay a while, I'll play a song for you." He began to tune the instrument. "What do you like? Blues? Jazz? Classical?"

"You can play classical guitar?"

"Sort of."

He played the hauntingly beautiful Sonata in E Minor by Scarlatti. Margaret Leigh was enthralled. When the last chord had died away, she stared at him a moment, speechless.

Then she spoke, her voice whispery with awe. "That was the most beautiful thing I've ever heard."

"Aw, shucks, ma'am." Andrew gave a good imitation of shuffling his feet and acting modest, but she could tell he was pleased.

"Why, Andrew, you could go on stage. You could record. You could leave all this behind." Her arm swept wide to encompass his cabin with the plain wooden floors and the simple chintz curtain.

"Why would I want to leave all this behind?"

"You could really make something of yourself, Andrew."

"I consider myself a finished product. I have no intention of changing—for anybody."

The hard, cold edge to his voice stopped her. She glanced at his face. Gone was the happy-little-boy look. Gone was the eagerness to please her.

"I'm sorry. I guess I got carried away." She stood up. "If you'll let me check on Christine, I'll be going."

His first instinct was to let her go. Good riddance. He liked variety, but not complications. And she was definitely complicating his life. But there was a certain gentle gallantry in him that didn't want her to leave while there were bad feelings between them.

"Don't go." Andrew came to her, his bare feet

padding on the floor and his guitar slapping his hip. "Not like this."

"Why should I stay?"

"Because of my famous charm?" He smiled at her.

She smiled back. "I shouldn't have said that about you making something of yourself. Its my upbringing, I guess. I come from a family who values achievement." She squeezed her hands together. "It's none of my business if you want to live in the woods with bird dogs."

He went very still, then blinked once, his eyes an icy blue. "They are nicer than some people I know."

Tension squeezed Margaret Leigh's chest. Her head felt light.

"I'll get your dog." Andrew spun on his heels and left the room. He knew the value of a timely exit.

He disappeared, and she stood in his den mentally kicking herself. The clock on the wall ticked loudly, keeping time with her thumping heart. She looked around at his simple abode. It had a rugged sort of charm, like the man who lived there. The couch was old but serviceable, the rocking chair was battered, and the tables were plain and sturdy. The room had the uncluttered look of having been decorated by a man who disdained material possessions.

Why on earth had she ever come? Because he had taken her dancing once and it had gone to her head? And whatever had prompted her to make that remark about his lack of ambition? It was true that he wouldn't fit in with her ambitious family, but he wasn't auditioning for the part. She had best see Christine and leave quickly, before she made a complete fool of herself.

Andrew returned, bearing a sleepy Christine. He handed the dog to Margaret Leigh, careful not to make physical contact.

Holding her dog next to her cheek, Margaret Leigh half turned so her back was to Andrew, but she could feel the heat of his gaze. It set prickles dancing along the back of her neck. Anxious to leave the charged atmosphere, she made her visit short.

"Bye, Christine. Be good." She kissed the poodle's nose and handed her back to Andrew. "Thanks for bringing her out." She backed around the rocking chair. "Good-bye, Andrew."

"I don't suppose you're planning to kiss my nose too?" His words were teasing, but his voice was cold.

She caught her lower lip between her teeth. With Andrew, she never quite knew what to say. She took the safe way. She said nothing. Instead, she waved one hand and quickly made her way out the door.

Andrew stood at his window and watched until her car had disappeared into the darkness. Christine wiggled and thumped her tail on his chest.

"Before we got into that brawl, she'd halfway invited me to dinner." He scratched the little dog's belly. "That's all I need—half an invitation."

He set Christine on the sofa and picked up the telephone. After three rings, his brother answered.

"Rick, I need a favor."

"Can you speak up, Andrew? The boys are making more noise than your dogs."

In the background Andrew could hear the triplets yelling, playing cowboys and Indians, no doubt, maybe even scalping each other with rubber knives. He chuckled. Rick's boys were hellions.

"There's going to be a family dinner in Tupelo.

It could be Jones, but it might be Adams. Find out when and where."

"I don't have to do any sleuthing to tell you that. Everybody knows that Governor Ben Adams is coming to town tomorrow to see his family. Bel Air Center. Tomorrow night at seven."

"News like that takes a while to get to Boguefala Bottom."

"Any special reason you want to know?"

"Yes. I need to prove something to a lady I know."

When Andrew walked into the Bel Air Center at seven-fifteen on Monday evening, the first person he saw was Margaret Leigh. She was talking with Governor Ben Adams and his lovely wife. Andrew knew Kate Adams from her pictures in the paper. As the mayor of Saltillo, she was famous for juggling a political career and a marriage to the governor.

But it was not the famous politicians who drew his attention; it was Margaret Leigh. She was dressed in a soft-looking red wool dress, and she was wearing her hair loose. He liked to think that was his influence.

He quickly made his way through the crowd. Margaret Leigh had her back to him, still talking to the governor.

"Hello, pretty one."

One hand flew to her cheek as she spun around. "Andrew. What in the world . . .?"

"I accepted your kind invitation." He made his way into the circle, slid one arm around her waist, and shook Ben Adams's hand.

"Hello, Governor Adams. Andrew McGill. Nice family you have."

"I think so." Ben touched Kate's elbow. "Have you met my wife, Kate?"

Margaret Leigh felt as if a circus with sixteen tigers and a full band had marched into the midst of the Adams family dinner. And one of those tigers had her in his grip. She was vividly aware of Andrew, of the heat and weight of his arm, of the size of him, of the fresh pine needles and sunshine smell of him, of the polished gold beauty of him. She wasn't aware of what he was saying, only of the way he charmed Ben and Kate Adams.

"So, there's a governor in your family?"

She came out of her trance and noticed that Ben and Kate had gone. "Yes. He's a third cousin. They have three children, Jane by her first marriage, then Ben, Jr., and Betsy." She was chattering, but she couldn't seem to help herself. "Jane's at Vanderbilt School of Law now."

"Introduce me around, Margaret Leigh. I want to meet all the family achievers."

"You're still mad about what I said yesterday."

"I never get mad, Margaret Leigh. I just get even."

"How did you know where to find me?"

"Clairvoyance. I have built-in radar that tracks you. My heart to yours." He placed a palm over the front of her dress, right over her heart. It thudded heavily against his hand.

"Remove your hand."

"You don't like it?" He grinned wickedly.

"Everybody's looking."

"Then maybe we should give them something to look at."

He bent over and kissed her, in front of God and the entire Adams family. He didn't pull her into a tight embrace or try to hold her embarrassingly close, but he did kiss her thoroughly, moving his lips over hers until he had elicited a response. When she was beginning to forget the circumstances and enjoy the contact, he pulled away.

Two distant cousins applauded. The rest of the family kept on talking.

Margaret Leigh put a trembling hand over her lips. "What are you trying to do? Start a family scandal?"

"My family doesn't consider kissing scandalous. I come from a family who values warmth and fun and spontaneity and happiness."

"Did you have to wait until tonight to tell me that? Why didn't you do it yesterday?"

"I wanted witnesses. Revenge is no fun without witnesses."

"You're going to drive me to cuss, Andrew McGill."

"Go ahead, Margaret Leigh. I don't think you'll scandalize anybody."

"Hell."

"Bravo. That's a beginning."

She drew herself up to her full height and looked him straight in the eye. "I consider myself a finished product, Andrew McGill. I don't need you to make me over."

They stared at each other for a moment. Andrew was the first to speak. "Guilty." His eyes crinkled with laughter. "I guess we're both guilty. From the minute I set eyes on you, I've tried to make you over."

"At least you're honest."

"So are you. Brave too. Not every woman can hold out against the famous McGill charm."

"I guess I'm not like every woman."

He studied her a long time, taking in the proud

tilt of her chin, her unwavering stare, the genuine goodness she wore like a second skin.

"No, you're not, Margaret Leigh." He tipped her chin up with one finger. "I think you're kind of special."

"No man has ever said that to me before."

"I'm glad I was your first."

She blushed. He held onto her chin a moment longer, drawing his thumb over her soft lower lip.

"I got what I came for. Whoever said 'Revenge is sweet' is right. It was mighty sweet, pretty one." He released her and took a step back. "I guess I'll be going, unless you want to invite me to stay for dinner."

"Stay for dinner, Andrew."

"That's a great idea, Margaret Leigh. I'm glad you thought of it."

Margaret Leigh watched him all through dinner. He had Aunt Bertha simpering and Aunt Grace giggling. He was funny when he wanted to be and serious when he needed to be. He did more than hold his own with her distant cousins who had distinguished themselves in the fields of medicine, law, and education: He shone. He was quick-witted, well read, and versatile.

Her face burned when she thought of labeling him as a man who lived in the woods with his dogs. A simple life didn't mean a simple mind.

Shortly after the meal, he took his leave. Margaret Leigh walked him to the double glass doors of the center.

"I'm glad you came, Andrew. I don't like to have misunderstandings . . . with anyone."

"Neither do I." He reached out and slid his

knuckles gently down the side of her face. "Take care, pretty one."

She stood at the door watching him. He was only a large shadow in the dark, but she watched anyway. Then she turned slowly and went toward the bathroom, wondering if she'd ever see him again. Of course, she'd see him when she picked up Christine, but that was different. Would he ask her to dance again? Would he linger on her front porch with his eyes of blue diamonds and his touch like flames?

She guessed not. Not only were they opposites in every way, they had hurt each other. And hurts were sometimes hard to heal.

She slipped into the bathroom stall and shut the door.

"Did you see that gorgeous hunk?"

Margaret Leigh recognized the voice. It was her third cousin, Suelynn Adams Green. She had two major achievements in life—being born with blond hair and marrying well. Her husband, Mack Green, was a surgeon.

"Good Lord, yes. What does a man like that see in a mousy little thing like Margaret Leigh?"

The other speaker was Glenny Adams, known among the clan as Jaws—sharp-tongued and vicious and vainglorious over being the daughter of the best criminal attorney in Mississippi.

Margaret Leigh stood very still. She didn't want to eavesdrop, but neither did she want to embarrass them and herself by making her presence known.

"It's a pity she doesn't look more like Tess. Now, there's a real beauty."

"My dear. Don't you know the family secret?" Glenny paused to give her a braying laugh. "They're not sisters."

Blood roared in Margaret Leigh's ears, shutting out all sound. A wave of nausea washed over her, and she leaned over the toilet, heaving silently. The green enamel on the walls swam before her eyes, and she knelt, gripping the edges of the toilet bowl.

"I will not faint," she whispered. "I will not faint."

Outside the stall she heard flushing toilets and clicking high heels. Then the banging of the bathroom door.

She stood up to leave. *They're not sisters.* The words screamed through her mind, over and over. She pressed her hands over her ears to shut out the sound.

Her legs went rubbery, and she sank onto the toilet seat. *They're not sisters.* The words ripped through her again, tearing out her heart, her spirit, her will. She huddled there, head on her knees, arms wrapped tightly around herself. She feared if she moved she would break.

Time dissolved. She let herself float in the void.

"Margaret Leigh." It was Aunt Bertha. "Margaret Leigh, honey. Are you in here?"

Margaret Leigh didn't have the energy to move. She closed her eyes and tried to shut out all sound.

"Grace said you came in here about thirty minutes ago." Aunt Bertha got down on her arthritic old knees and peeped under the stalls. She saw her niece's shoes. "Come on out, honey."

Margaret Leigh rose slowly and pushed open the door. She didn't even know if she had any right to call the woman in front of her *aunt*.

"Good Lord. You're as white as a sheet. Are you sick?"

"Yes." She took her aunt's arm, as much for support as anything. "Let's go home."

"Let me get my purse."

They drove home in silence. In the dim light of the dashboard, Margaret Leigh looked pinched and drawn, fifteen years older than she was.

Habit carried Margaret Leigh through. Habit helped her park the car, walk up the porch steps, and unlock her door. Out of habit she went into the den, turned on a lamp, and found a chair.

Aunt Bertha hovered in the doorway, anxious and frightened. "Maybe you should go to bed, honey."

"We need to talk."

Aunt Bertha twisted her hands together. "You probably ate something that made you sick."

"No, I *heard* something that made me sick." Margaret Leigh lifted her head and looked at her aunt with huge, stricken eyes. "Is Tess my sister?"

Aunt Bertha went pale. She pressed one trembling hand over her heart and caught the doorsill with the other.

Margaret Leigh squeezed her thighs together and pressed her arms hard against her side. Fear filled her.

"Is Tess my sister?" she repeated. "Is she?" The sound of her own voice was harsh in her ears. She seemed to float out of her own body and look down on the rising hysteria of the woman huddled below her. "*Is she?*"

"Oh, dear Lord in heaven. What have I done?" Aunt Bertha bowed her head and let the tears rain down her cheeks—tears of guilt, tears of sorrow, and finally, after years of carrying the heavy burden—tears of release.

Five

Margaret Leigh rose from her chair, feeling like a sleepwalker. She gripped her aunt's shoulders.

"Aunt Bertha. Look at me. I have to know." She felt the shudder that ran through her aunt. "Is Tess my sister?"

Aunt Bertha lifted her tear-stained face. "No." She walked over to the sofa and sat down.

The truth made Margaret Leigh stronger. She paced the room, charged with restless energy and the need to understand.

"Why was it kept a secret? Adoption is no crime."

Aunt Bertha buried her face in her hands again and began to sob.

"Aunt Bertha?" She stopped beside the sofa and turned to face her aunt. "I assume I'm adopted. Or was Tess? Is Tess adopted?"

"No." Slowly Aunt Bertha lifted her head. The truth was out. There was nothing to do but try and make Margaret Leigh understand. "You were the one. You were the one born out of wedlock, born in secret and given to Margaret to raise as her own . . . She loved you. She was a good mother. You had a good home."

All the words Margaret Leigh was hearing sank in. *Born in secret. Given to Margaret.* The fear rose up again, threatening to smother her.

"Why was I born in secret, Aunt Bertha? Why was I given away?"

"You have to understand, Margaret Leigh. He was married . . ."

Aunt Bertha started sobbing again.

Margaret Leigh sank onto the sofa. The truth hung over the room like an ugly pall. Everything she'd believed in had crumbled at her feet. Everything she had lived was a lie.

"Who is my mother?"

Aunt Bertha cried louder.

"Aunt Bertha." Margaret Leigh rose from the sofa, gripping the arms for support. *"Who is my mother?"*

A shudder went through Aunt Bertha. When she lifted her face, Margaret Leigh saw death.

"I am."

The words exploded inside Margaret Leigh. Aunt Bertha, who had preached virtue and goodness, who had railed against scoundrels and sin. Aunt Bertha, who had brought her up to be almost an ice maiden—Aunt Bertha was not her aunt at all. Aunt Bertha was her mother.

Rage came on the heels of shock. Margaret Leigh threw back her shoulders like a soldier going into battle. Then she marched from the room.

"Margaret Leigh," Bertha called after her. "Where are you going?"

"I'm going to sin."

"Wait. Let me explain."

Margaret Leigh ran out the door and down the

front steps. Blindly, she climbed into her car and turned the key. She was Bertha Adam's bastard. Conceived in sin. Born in secret. She didn't need any explanations. She didn't want any excuses. Lies. Everything in her life had been lies. She wasn't even Margaret Leigh Jones. She was an Adams. And Lord only knew what else.

She gunned the engine and drove away from the house. It didn't even seem like her house anymore. Nothing seemed real. Where had all her virtue gotten her? Nowhere. Like mother, like daughter. She might as well go out and vamp the whole damned town.

Her knuckles turned white on the wheel, and she found herself heading out of town. Where did a woman go to sin? She supposed most women knew at least a dozen places, a dozen ways, a dozen men. But she knew only one—Andrew McGill.

His house was dark when she arrived. She didn't care. She walked up the steps and knocked on his door. She didn't wait for an answer but knocked and knocked until her knuckles were bleeding.

Suddenly the door opened, and Andrew was there in bare feet and tight jeans, running a hand through his disheveled hair.

"Margaret Leigh. What in the devil . . .?" Her eyes were huge. She just stood on his front porch, gazing at him with those purple eyes. He took her elbow and gently drew her into the cabin. "Is someone sick? Is it your aunt?"

Margaret Leigh blinked at him slowly, and then she smiled. "My aunt? My aunt!" She threw back her head and laughed. The sound sent shivers down Andrew's spine.

"Come over here, Margaret Leigh, and sit down." He led her to the sofa and drew her down, keeping his arm around her shoulders. One hand massaged her upper arm, back and forth, up and down, over and over, touching, comforting. "Where's your coat? Did you forget your coat, sweetheart?"

"No. I didn't forget anything."

Her breathing was shallow, and she stared straight ahead as if she were seeing something that he could not.

"I'm glad you came to me." He moved his hand to her back, keeping up the massage, kneading the stiff muscles in her shoulders, caressing the tense line of her back. "I'm a good listener, and I'm a pretty good fixer." Silence from Margaret Leigh. "I have a sister and a brother, you know. Rick was always an independent cuss, but Jo Beth was a little blond slip of girl who was always getting into trouble." A shudder went through Margaret Leigh. Andrew kept talking and caressing. "One time she climbed into the orchard next door to our house and stole some little green apples. She ate until she got sick. I took the punishment for her. I marched next door, holding my baseball cap in my hands, looking contrite, and I apologized to old man Clifford for stealing his apples." A soft sigh from Margaret Leigh. A slight relaxing. Andrew rubbed and talked, keeping his voice low and singsong, like music. "He was a mean old cuss. Always looking over the fence and threatening to tell on us. Of course, Jo Beth and I deserved to be told on. We were always getting into mischief."

Margaret Leigh slumped against him, letting her head loll on his shoulder. "Keep talking."

"She's married now, married to a doctor in San Francisco. Colter Gray Wolf. He's Apache, a terrific athlete, and a fine horseman. We don't see them much. They'll come, though, after the babies are born. She's pregnant. Twins, the doctor says. They're trying to catch up with Rick and his wife, Martha Ann. They have two sets of triplets, three boys and three girls." Margaret Leigh burrowed closer to him, circling her arm over his chest. He held her tighter. "Any day now I'll be an uncle again. Always an uncle, never a father."

Margaret Leigh stirred. Slowly she sat up. Her eyes were bright and her face was flushed.

"I'll make you a father."

"What?"

"I said, I'll make you a father. I'll have your baby."

"Good Lord! What in the devil are you talking about?"

Her lips trembled. "You don't want me?"

He studied her through narrowed eyes. Something was going on. And he was going to find out. "What are we talking about here? Marriage or sex?"

"Sex."

He didn't blink an eye. He sat on the sofa pretending that the prim Miss Margaret Leigh Jones talked about sex every morning before breakfast and three times a day thereafter.

"You want to make love?" She didn't move. "Is that why you came out here, Margaret Leigh? To make love with me?"

She took a deep breath. "It's not love I want to make. It's lust." She leaned closer. "Say you want me, Andrew."

"I want you."

"Then take me."

"Do you know what you're asking?"

"I'm not asking for the moon, just a little old-fashioned sin."

"Loving is not a sin."

"The way I plan to do it, it is."

She looped one arm around his neck and drew his head down to hers. Her lips were hot on his, burning, seeking, eager. Some sane part of his mind told him to pull away. Alarm bells sounded throughout his system. But with Margaret Leigh's mouth on his, he couldn't think rationally.

She was inexperienced. He could tell that. But she was willing to learn. No. More than willing. Desperate.

He fitted Margaret Leigh against him, kissing her deep and long and hard, doing what he'd wanted to do since the night she'd gone dancing in her blue taffeta dress. She was limp and pliant in his arms—too limp, too pliant.

He pressed his hands tightly against her back, and he could feel the slight tremors that ran through her. Gentling her with his hands, his mouth, he sought to comfort with touch, to heal with kisses.

He had no intention of taking her into his bedroom. Not tonight. Maybe not ever. Not that she wasn't desirable. Not that he didn't want her. But he had a certain code of honor he lived by, tarnished though it might be. When he mated with a woman, he did it out of love, not lust. That didn't mean he was altarbound with every woman he took to his bed. But he did feel a certain kind of love, a compelling need.

Margaret Leigh clung to him, her mouth open and receptive. She was sweet, sweeter than he'd imagined. With the smell of roses and lilacs in her hair and the taste of honey in her mouth, she was a tempting morsel. He felt himself drifting toward the edge of no return.

He broke contact and lifted his head. Her face was wet with tears.

"You're crying." He touched her cheek gently, as if too much handling would shatter her.

She snuffled and tried to smile. "I don't care. Kiss me."

He brushed his lips across her cheek.

"Not like that." She grabbed his upper arms, her fingernails bit into his flesh.

His gaze swung from her face to her hands.

"Good Lord. You're bleeding."

He pried one of her hands loose and held it, examining her knuckles. The skin was scratched and torn, bloody in places.

"What in the hell have you done?"

"You're cussing. I've never heard you cuss."

"It's cussing time." He grabbed her other hand. It was the same, battered and bleeding. She tried to pull away, but he held her fast. "Are you going to tell me what's going on?"

"I didn't come here to talk." Her hands clenched into tight fists. "I don't want to talk."

He studied her closely then, examined the bright glazed eyes, noticed the shallow breathing. Discreetly he slid two fingers over her wrist. Her pulse was racing. He was no doctor, but he'd heard enough medical talk from his brother-in-law to guess that Margaret Leigh was close to shock. What do you do for somebody in shock? Keep them warm and quiet, he decided. But first he needed to take care of her hands.

"Wait right here, Margaret Leigh."

He put a sofa pillow behind her back and

propped her up like a broken doll. All the life seemed to have gone out of her.

"Where are you going?"

"To get bandages for your hands." He stood up, keeping his movements easy and his voice low. "Stay right here. Don't move. I'll be right back."

He hurried into his bathroom, gathering what he needed as quickly as possible. When he returned Margaret Leigh was exactly as he had left her, propped on the pillows, one hand on her knee and one lying on the sofa.

Her eyes flickered when he sat down beside her, but she didn't seem to be seeing him. He cleansed her wounds, then applied antibiotic salve and bandages, handling her as he would a newborn puppy. She was just about as helpless.

When he had finished, he set the supplies aside and took her hands in his.

"Margaret Leigh, I don't think you should drive. I'm going to take you home."

"No!" She bolted from the sofa and began to pace. "I'm not going home. I can't go back. I don't even have a home. Not anymore. I can't go. . . . I can't face her. . . . I can't—"

"All right. It's okay." Andrew went to her and pulled her into his arms, pressing her trembling body close against him.

"There now. Shh. It's all right." He stroked her back, her hair, her arms, over and over. "You don't have to go. You can stay here. Shh. It's all right now."

Gradually she began to relax. With a sigh, she leaned into his embrace.

"I have an extra bedroom. You can sleep there." She nodded, and he kept up the tender massage. Who did she not want to face? What had happened to make her think she no longer had a home? He approached the subject with caution.

"Is there anyone you want to call?"

"No." Her vehement answer shook him. He remembered Saturday night and her request to leave the dance early in order to see about Aunt Bertha. Nothing added up. But it was the wrong time to find answers.

"It's getting late," he said. "Why don't we go to bed? Sometimes a good night's sleep lends perspective to problems."

She didn't comment but allowed herself to be led to his spare bedroom like a trusting child.

"I think I have an old T-shirt around here that will do for a nightgown. I'll be right back.

He went across the hall and dug in his closet for an oversized T-shirt with a Mississippi State logo, a big maroon bulldog snarling against a white background. At least it used to be white. Age and too many careless washings had turned the shirt a dingy yellow. It wasn't pretty, but it was soft and warm and serviceable.

When he reentered the bedroom, she was standing exactly where he had left her. She was like a statue. Wherever he placed her, that's where she stayed.

He held the shirt out to her. "Margaret Leigh, here's your nightshirt." She made absolutely no response. He tossed the shirt onto the bed. "Turn around, sweetheart. I'm going to unzip your dress."

She did—slowly, as if she were performing a chore she had almost forgotten how to do. He lowered her zipper and slid her dress down her shoulders. Her skin had the fair and tender look of never having been exposed to the sun. Andrew resisted the temptation to run his hands down the length of that soft, inviting expanse of skin.

Think of her as your sister, he told himself. The admonition helped, but not much. He guided the dress downward, over her flat stomach, down her slender legs, until it pooled like wine at her feet. Underneath, she was wearing a peach-colored silk slip. No lace, no fancy trimmings, just a simple garment that hugged her body in all the right places.

She had an elegant body, the kind that went with long legs and an Audrey Hepburn neck. Another time he'd have lingered over it; he'd have appreciated it with his hands and his lips as well as his eyes.

Tonight he merely took note.

"Are you all right, sweetheart?"

There was no reply. A shudder passed through Margaret Leigh, and she wrapped her arms around herself.

"Are you cold?"

She shook her head, but he wasn't sure whether what he had said had registered with her. He thought of picking her up and tucking her into bed as she was, but he knew enough about women's lingerie to know that sleeping in a bra would be uncomfortable.

"I'm going to take off your slip now, Margaret Leigh."

She looked at her dress on the floor with the same curious detachment she might have given a passing bug. It didn't seem to have any connection with her.

Andrew felt another shiver run through her when he put his hands on her shoulders. Her skin was warm to his touch. It wasn't the cold that made her shiver, he decided. It was fear.

"What are you afraid of, Margaret Leigh? I'm not going to hurt you."

She lifted wounded violet eyes to his, but still she said nothing. He had seen that look on the face of mothers with sick children and on widows. Without another word, he circled his arms around her and held her close. It was a warm and friendly embrace, a hug of affirmation, a touch of compassion.

She stood stiffly in his arms, and then she leaned her cheek against his bare shoulder. He cupped the back of her head, sinking his fingers into the heavy silk of her hair.

"Do you want to tell me about it, sweetheart?"

"No."

He could barely hear her, even in the silence of the room.

"That's all right. I'll be here all night, just across the hall. If you need me, all you have to do is give a yell. I'm well trained. I'll come running."

She made a quiet sound, like the whisper of wind through willows. Then she gave a small nod.

Everything about her was fragile, her cheek against his chest, her hand resting in the crook of his elbow, her emotions. He didn't know what would happen if he finished undressing her. And now was not the time to find out. Comfort would have to take a backseat to common sense. And common sense told him to get her into bed, settled and warm, as quickly as possible.

"I'm going to put you to bed now, Margaret Leigh."

She nodded again, a small motion that caused her silky hair to brush against his cheek. He held onto her with one hand and reached for the nightshirt with the other.

"Lift your arms." She did as she was told. He

slid the shirt over her head, working her hands and arms through the armholes. Her arms stayed stiffly in the air until he caught her wrists and lowered them to her sides.

"There. That should keep you warm and comfortable." He kept up a steady, reassuring stream of chatter as he picked her up. She was limp and lifeless, without resistance, almost without a will. "This bed has an old feather mattress. I used to love these things when I was a kid. Still do."

He braced one knee on the bed, and the bedsprings squeaked. Margaret Leigh clung to him, hiding her face in the crook of his neck. He started to lower her to the bed, then he noticed the bedcovers weren't turned back. He didn't want to disturb her by putting her down again. Balancing her with one free arm and his knee, he managed the covers with his free hand.

It was awkward, but it worked. He lowered her gently to the sheets. She sank into the feather mattress, sighing. He arranged the covers over her with great care, tucking the blanket around her legs and snugging it closely under her chin. When he had finished, he bent down and kissed her forehead.

"Sleep tight, pretty one."

Margaret Leigh's gaze held him. Her eyes were bright with unshed tears and huge with pain. He tenderly brushed her hair back from her forehead.

"Everything will be all right, Margaret Leigh. Just you wait and see."

"Thank you, Andrew." He could barely hear her whisper.

"You're more than welcome."

He left her bed and moved quietly about the room, doing small things that would make the bedroom a haven for her. He got a night-light off the closet shelf and plugged it in. Then he picked her dress off the floor, smoothed it down, and draped it neatly over the back of a chair. After he had done all that, he flicked the light off, left the room, and closed the door.

He stood outside her door for a long while, listening for any sound. When he was satisfied that she wasn't going to try to leave, he went across the hall to his own bedroom. Leaving his own door open, he stripped quickly and climbed into bed. The sheets felt cool and crisp. He punched his pillow twice, an old habit of his, and was just turning onto his stomach for a good night's sleep when he remembered his nakedness. What if he had to rush across the hall in the middle of the night? It wouldn't do to rescue Margaret Leigh buck naked. She was a lady, even if she had tried to seduce him.

He climbed out of bed and slipped back into his shorts. He felt as bundled up and restricted as if he were wearing an expedition outfit for the North Pole, but he was willing to make the sacrifice. After all, it wasn't every evening a man was called on to be a hero. He laced his hands behind his head and lay back on his pillow, staring into the dark. There was something heroic about being the one Margaret Leigh had turned to in her time of trouble. He felt about ten feet tall.

What in the devil was bothering her? What had sent her flying into the night?

His mind tried to latch onto some clue she had dropped, but he found himself drifting into sleep, lulled by the sound of pines whispering outside his window and the far-off call of a whippoorwill.

The sobs woke Andrew up. At first he was disoriented, then he came fully alert. He leaped out of bed and raced across the hall.

Margaret Leigh was huddled in the middle of the bed, her knees drawn up to her chest and her arms around her legs, as she rocked back and forth and cried.

"Margaret Leigh," he called from the door.

She made no answer. In fact, she didn't even look his way.

"I heard you crying." He approached the bed with caution. He didn't want to say or do anything to upset her even more. "Is there anything I can do to help?"

"I want the world to come to an end." She lifted her tear-streaked face to his. "Can you bring the world to an end, Andrew?"

Andrew McGill was a man of action. Furthermore, he knew that drastic need called for drastic measures. He threw back the covers and climbed into bed with her.

He pried her hands away from her legs and unfolded her like a pretzel. Then he wrapped her in his strong embrace and lay down with her.

"I can't bring the world to an end, Margaret Leigh, and in the morning, you'll be glad I couldn't." He spoke in the matter-of-fact tone his parents had used with him when he'd had some childish notion that the problems of the moment would last forever. "Now, just put your head on my shoulder." He felt her stiffen as her mood took a one-hundred-and-eighty-degree turn from sadness to anger. Then she was shoving him, pushing his chest with the strength born of rage. He held her tight. "No, don't struggle against me, sweetheart. I'm too big and strong for you. I'll win every time."

"You didn't want me . . . I offered myself and you refused."

"You would have hated me in the morning. Be still, Margaret Leigh."

She fought with hands and knees, clawing at his back and shoulders. And she was stronger than she looked.

"Good Lord, woman." He bowed his back to get out of the way of her lethal knee.

"Get out of my bed."

"It's not your bed, sweetheart. It's mine."

She was still for a moment, and he thought she was calming down. Then she started struggling again. He was glad. Her limp defeat had been frightening. Her rage would be cathartic.

"You beast. You blackguard." Her fists had all the impact of a mosquito battling a tough-skinned rhinoceros, but her fingernails were drawing blood. "What kind of man are you? Refusing the request of a lady?"

"Ahhh, a lady, are you?" He caught her flailing fists and pinned them to the bed. "No lady I ever knew has a right hook like yours."

She jacked her knees up again, and Andrew rolled on top of her. He braced her arms above her head and straddled her hips.

"Fight, pretty one. Get all that rage out of your system."

"Rage is not how I plan to get this out of my system." She bucked under him. "Let go of me."

"How do you plan to get it out?"

"Sex."

"Some other time, pretty lady."

"Not with you, you backwoods Romeo."

She twisted her head and took a bite out of his upper arm. He felt the pain of her teeth, but he kept his hold. He even managed a chuckle.

"I am that, my love. And more. Maybe someday I'll show you."

"Put your money where your mouth is."

She bucked against him again. It was almost more than he could take. Anger was always stimulating, and that natural stimulation combined with the proximity of her body already had him in a state that couldn't be disguised. He was almost tempted to give her what she wanted. But he knew it was an action he'd regret. No, more than regret. If he made love to Margaret Leigh in her condition, he could never again call himself honorable.

"Not tonight, sweetheart. Tonight, all I want to do is keep you from leaving here and doing something foolish."

"A woman on the hunt is foolish? How about a man on the hunt?"

"Hungry."

"Show me."

"Dammit, Margaret Leigh."

"Show me."

His mouth slammed down on hers. And still she fought. They rolled across the bed together, mouths locked and legs entangled. It was a battle of wills. Both were determined to win.

Margaret Leigh didn't know the first thing about seducing a man, but she gave it her best shot. She pressed herself into Andrew McGill's big muscular body, teasing him with inviting little movements of her hips.

She was a natural, and just didn't know it. Andrew clamped down on his control, fighting the raging passion that threatened to take them both over the edge. He thought that if he kissed her long enough, she'd settle down and listen to reason.

She thought if she kissed him long enough, he'd surrender and give her what she wanted. She wanted to have sex. She didn't want love or tenderness or caring or even passion. She wanted to crawl in the gutter and have sex. Any old body would do. But Andrew McGill would do better than most.

She rubbed herself against him, hating what she was doing but doing it anyhow. When had she crossed the threshold from heart-broken to enraged? And how many times had she crossed it? Her emotions were swinging wildly. She was on a merry-go-round and couldn't seem to get off. Nor did she want to. If she got off, she'd have to face the truth. And the truth hurt too much. It was far, far better for her to drown the truth in decadence. Like mother, like daughter.

Once, when his hands glided tenderly down her back and his mouth promised heaven, she almost backed down, she almost rolled her face into the pillow and let the tears come. Andrew had been good to her, kind, considerate, sweet, generous. And he had taken her in, patched her hands, then undressed her and offered his bed.

No. She wouldn't let herself get soft and sentimental. From now on she would be as tough as nails. She'd be cynical and hard, and she'd sin like the very devil. She was finished with trust, through with caution, disgusted with purity.

Andrew came up for air, his hold loosening. She took the opportunity to sit up and strip the T-shirt over her head. He grabbed her arm.

"What the devil are you doing?"

"I don't intend to do it for the first time with my clothes on."

"Dammit, Margaret Leigh."

She glared at him. In the dim glow of the night-light he could see the determination on her face. With one quick movement he divested himself of his shorts. She sucked in her breath in shock, then she averted her eyes.

He could have gotten onto his knees and praised all the saints for that one small gesture, that one hint that Margaret Leigh wasn't quite the brazen hussy she was pretending to be. But he had better things to do.

He reached for her.

"You've finally come to your senses, have you?" She came to him willingly.

"I certainly have." He twisted his shorts into a rope and looped them around her wrist.

'What are you doing?"

"Taking you captive, my dear."

He placed his wrist on top of hers and bound the two together with his boxer shorts. It was a tight squeeze, but he managed to tie a knot that would hold.

"Why, you—"

"Lie down and be quiet, Margaret Leigh. I'm going to sleep." He stretched out, naked as the day he was born, and shut his eyes. "I have bird dogs to train in the morning."

She thought of putting up another fight, but all the energy seemed to have gone out of her. She lay down beside him, keeping as much distance between her body and his as she could possibly manage. Then she tried to sleep.

Six

The morning sun streaming through the window woke Andrew. The first thing he did was turn his head to check his captive. Margaret Leigh was on her side, her back to him, her free hand under her cheek and one knee drawn up to her stomach. Her slip straps had slid off her shoulders, revealing the lacy bra underneath. Her thick, silky hair was deliciously tumbled, and long lashes fanned across her sleep-rosy cheeks.

All that could have been mine, he thought as he quietly slid his hand out of the bonds and eased off the bed. She didn't even stir. She was exhausted, ravaged, no doubt, by her emotions.

Outside he could hear his dogs baying, greeting the morning sun and reminding him it was time for breakfast. He hurried from the room and closed the door softly behind him. She would sleep till he got back. Then when she woke up, he and Miss Margaret Leigh Jones were going to have a long talk.

* * *

Margaret Leigh woke up with a start. The sun slanted across her eyes, and for a moment she thought she was in her own bed. The dull throbbing in her head and the heaviness in her body quickly vanquished that dream. She would never have another ordinary morning as long as she lived.

She sat up, holding her head and groaning. The shorts dangling from her wrist brushed against her cheek. She jerked them off and threw them across the room. They landed in the corner and lay in a heap like an accusing eye, mocking her. Andrew's shorts were a vivid reminder of what had taken place in that bed.

Her face burning, she jumped up and looked at the rumpled sheets. She had thrown herself at Andrew like some brassy wench, and he had turned her down. Humiliation crushed her, making it difficult to breathe.

She had to get out of there. She had to leave before she made a fool of herself all over again. Where was her dress? She didn't even remember getting out of it. She turned slowly and saw it draped over a chair. Picking it up, she saw the bandages on her hands. She had forgotten about them. Andrew had put them there. Always Andrew.

She struggled with her dress, feeling weak and too tired to raise the zipper.

"I'll help you with that."

She whirled at the sound of Andrew's voice. He was standing in the doorway, casually offering his help as if he hadn't turned her down then climbed buck naked into her bed and tied her up with his underwear.

Rage and humiliation almost choked her.

"If you ever touch me again, I'll wrap your family jewels around your neck and hang you with them."

He chuckled. "I'm glad to see you're feeling better this morning." He strolled into the room and moved her trembling hands away from her zipper. Then he fastened her dress as if it were his right.

"Leave me alone." She jerked out of his reach.

He crossed back to the doorway and leaned there, standing guard.

"You look pale today, Margaret Leigh. You should still be in bed."

"I wouldn't get into your bed if it were the last place on earth to put my head."

"Anger is a good sign that you're healing."

"There's nothing to heal." She combed her hair with her fingers, making herself ready to leave. "Move out of my way."

"Where are you going?"

"Why do you care?"

"You came to me. Remember?"

She remembered only too well. Tears stung the back of her eyelids, but she held them in.

Andrew crossed the room swiftly. His hands were gentle as they bracketed her shoulders.

"You can stay here as long as you need to, Margaret Leigh. If you want to talk, I'll listen, and if you want to keep quiet, I won't pry." He tipped her chin up with one finger. "Let me be your friend, sweetheart."

"I don't need a friend. I need a lover." She shoved against him and marched out of the room.

He thought about calling her back, but he knew it would be useless. And he didn't intend to keep her there by force. He stood in the bedroom until he heard his front door slam, then he walked into his den and looked out the window. Her head was high as she climbed into her car.

"She'll make it. She'll be all right."

His words echoed in the quiet room, and he wondered why he was trying to reassure himself about Margaret Leigh's well being. Who was she to him? Just a lovely old-fashioned woman he'd taken dancing. It was best altogether to let her go.

He whistled as he turned to his kitchen to make breakfast. He'd always believed that a little music and a full stomach made it easier to face the day. He made scrambled eggs and toast, then he sliced bananas on his corn flakes and poured himself a big glass of orange juice, telling himself all the while that he had bird dogs to train. He couldn't be worrying about Margaret Leigh.

Margaret Leigh held the steering wheel in a death grip as she left behind the cabin in Boguefala Bottom. What was she going to do? She couldn't go to work looking the way she did, and she couldn't go home. Up ahead she spotted a service station. She pulled in and ducked into the ladies' room, taking the purse on the front seat of her car. It had stayed there all night, undisturbed.

She made repairs to her hair and face the best way she could, then she went inside and bought herself a candy bar and a soft drink. Breakfast. Yesterday she would never have dreamed of abusing her body with junk food. But this was another day. She might eat nothing but candy and soda for the rest of her life. It would serve Aunt Bertha right if she died of malnutrition—if she didn't die of humiliation first.

The day at the library was long, but then days

accompanied by anger and agony and guilt always were. Margaret Leigh brushed a strand of hair from her eyes as she placed a load of books on the book cart. A streak of late-afternoon sun slanted through the high windows on the west side of the processing department, setting dust motes dancing among the books waiting to be catalogued. The clock on the wall religiously guarded the time, doling it out with each revolution of the minute hand.

Margaret Leigh glanced at the clock. Five minutes to five. Only five more minutes and she could leave. But then what would she do? Where would she go?

"I'm glad you're alone, Margaret Leigh."

She jerked her head toward the door. Andrew McGill stood there in his leather jacket, looking as out of place among the books and paste as a wolf in a gathering of lambs. She groped for her tattered defenses and her wits at the same time.

"This is not the place to check out books. You'll have to go downstairs to the front desk."

"I'm not here to check out books."

She'd be darned if she'd ask him why he was there. She stayed where she was, glad the book cart was between them.

"I'm here to see if you're all right."

"I'm great. Top of the world. Free as a bird."

"Then why aren't you smiling?"

She bared her teeth at him. "I'm smiling."

"No, you're not. You're hurting."

"I don't want your pity."

"It's not pity; it's friendship."

She didn't want friendship. Friends trusted each other, and she would never trust again.

"Since you don't want my body, why do you want my friendship?"

"Dammit, Margaret Leigh. There's more to a man and a woman than sex."

"Not that I've noticed."

"Then you've been looking in the wrong places."

"Where should I look . . . the Pirates' Den?"

Guilty, Andrew thought. He was the one who had shown her that side of life, all under the guise of making her over. His plan had backfired. He stalked across the room, shoving the book cart aside and gripping her shoulders.

"I've never seen a woman so bent on destroying herself. Why are you doing this?"

"Why do you care?"

His face softened, and his hands began to make lazy circles on her upper arm.

"Darned if I know." If she had ever seen a more endearing smile, she didn't know where. She hardened her heart. "Maybe it's because I like to keep both the dogs I train and their owners happy." He brushed his knuckles down the side of her face. "Or maybe it's because you have such soft skin." His gaze held hers as he caressed her face with the back of his hand. "I asked myself that same question today. Why can't I just train my bird dogs and let you do whatever it is you're bound and determined to do?"

"Did you ever answer yourself?" She hated the way her voice had gone whispery and soft and the way she trembled inside, waiting for his reply. That was the old Margaret Leigh talking, the one who was too scared of men even to give them a decent kiss, the one who believed in the redemptive qualities of love. The new Margaret Leigh rose to the surface. She shoved his hands aside and stepped out of his range. "Not that I care, one way or the other."

Andrew crammed his hands into his pockets.

"Don't take anything personally. I guess I'm getting soft in my old age."

The hurt she felt was unexpected and unwelcome. She didn't have room in her life for any more pain. She had to get rid of this man once and for all. A wickedness born of desperation rose to her aid.

"I can vouch for that. You've gotten soft in more places than one."

He threw back his head and hooted with laughter. It wasn't the reaction she'd expected.

"If you keep issuing challenges like that, I'll be forced to prove you wrong."

"You had your chance and you blew it."

He studied her, his eyes as intense as the center of blue-hot flames. "What am I going to do with you?"

"Nothing. It's quitting time. I'm leaving." She picked up her purse and started toward the door.

"Where are you going? Home?"

She turned in the doorway. "That's none of your business, Andrew McGill."

"I'm making it my business."

"Then you should know this: I'm not the same woman who came to your cabin last Saturday. I'm a new flaming, sizzling Margaret Leigh. Don't come too close or you might get burned."

"I thrive on heat."

She slung her bag over her shoulder and marched from the processing room, her head high and her heels tapping an angry rhythm on the tile floor. Andrew didn't even bother to disguise his intent. He followed her, not caring if everybody in the library saw them.

Margaret Leigh heard his footsteps, as loud as doom, coming down the stairs behind her. She felt his large shadow as she passed through the front doors. She heard his truck shift into gear as she pulled out of the parking lot. Andrew McGill was a maniac. He was going to follow her all the way home.

Home. She got fainthearted just thinking about going back to the house on Allen Street. She had to go back sometime. What other choice did she have? She had no clothes except the ones on her back, and she had exactly thirty-two dollars and fifteen cents in her purse. Not enough for a decent motel room. And with Christmas coming soon, she didn't dare overload her credit card.

She saddened at the thought of Christmas. Who would she send gifts to this year? She didn't even know who were her real relatives.

Her steps dragged as she left her car and walked up her porch steps. It had taken all her energy to face down Andrew in the library. Out of the corner of her eye she could see his red truck, parked boldly at the curb. She hoped he got gray hairs from the boredom of waiting for her.

She pushed open the front door and slipped inside.

"Margaret Leigh. Is that you, honey?"

Bertha Adams appeared in the doorway of her bedroom. There were dark circles under her eyes, and her pink challis dress looked as if she'd slept in it.

Margaret Leigh squelched the quick surge of compassion. Old habits would die hard, but she was going to do her best to give them a quick and merciful death.

"Yes, it's me. But you needn't bother coming out. I won't be here long enough for a mother-daughter chat."

"Please." Bertha pulled at her frazzled gray hair. "Come inside and talk to me. Let me explain."

"You already have. You slept with another woman's husband, and when you found yourself in the unfortunate situation of being pregnant, you did the noble thing and gave me away."

"It wasn't like that. We loved each other. I love *you*." Bertha came out of her room and clutched at Margaret Leigh's sleeve. "You have to understand . . . I had no other choice."

"Leave us both some dignity. Please." She plucked the hand off her arm and continued up the stairs.

"Where are you going?"

"To pack a bag."

"You're going to Chicago? To stay with Tess?"

"No. I'm going to stay with the first man who will have me."

Bertha clutched her heart and grew faint. But a sudden burst of maternal love gave her courage. She forgot about her own health and started up the stairs after her daughter. At this moment, nothing was more important to her than Margaret Leigh. She braced herself in the doorway and stood watching her daughter cram clothes into her suitcase. She wasn't even bothering to fold them. That wasn't like Margaret Leigh. She'd always been so neat.

Bertha drew a big breath and starting talking, very fast. "I didn't think I could get pregnant. I was old, already in menopause. But it happened anyhow." She paused for breath, then hurried on. "In the sixties there was a stigma against women who got pregnant and didn't have husbands. Abortion was not a choice for me, and there were no homes for unwed mothers, not in Tupelo anyhow. An unmarried woman pregnant in the sixties was an outcast. The stigma was even worse for the child. They were called names."

"I know the name. Bastard."

Bertha ignored her. "Margaret knew she couldn't have other children. The doctor had said it would kill her. I couldn't go to . . . your father, so I went to her. She and Graham were living in South Carolina at the time. They wanted you. Cousin Joseph did the legal work."

Glenny's daddy. It fit, Margaret Leigh thought. *That's why Glenny knew the family secret.*

"We all agreed it would be best if you never knew."

"Best for whom? for you? for"—she couldn't bring herself to say "*Mother and Daddy*"—"Margaret and Graham Jones?" She snapped her suitcase shut. "I'm leaving. Don't bother waiting up for me."

"Where will you stay?" Bertha stepped aside as Margaret Leigh brushed past her. "Where did you stay last night? What did you do last night?" Icy silence and a retreating back were her only answers. "Be careful," she called after her daughter. The front door slammed behind Margaret Leigh. "Oh, honey, do be careful. Such bad things can happen to nice girls."

Bertha sank onto the floor and buried her face in her hands.

Andrew McGill hounded Margaret Leigh's steps. He followed her to Finney's Sandwich shop and sat across the aisle from her while she ate.

The red truck followed her up and down the streets as she wandered aimlessly, not knowing what to do, not even caring what she did. Once or twice she tried to lose him, but her heart wasn't in it. What did she care if he wasted his gas and his evening watchdogging her?

On impulse she drove to the theater and went inside. The movie was already in progress, but she didn't care about that either. The theater was dark, the movie was bad, and most of the seats were empty. Andrew sat two rows behind her. She didn't even have to turn her head to see him; she could feel his eyes boring into her back. She thought she heard him crunching popcorn. He was trying to build his energy, no doubt, for the formidable task ahead.

And she was darned sure going to make his task formidable. Not that she cared one way or the other what Andrew McGill thought. She didn't care what anybody thought. She wanted two things: revenge and lust.

She glanced down at her watch. It was nine o'clock. Just about time, she guessed, for a place like the Pirates' Den to be gearing up for the evening crowd.

She left her seat and quickly made her way out of the darkened theater.

Andrew sat on a bar stool and watched Margaret Leigh dance. She'd picked Hooter. Somehow he'd known she would. He nursed his root beer and brooded. He'd never been anybody's guardian angel except Jo Beth's, and that didn't count. He'd been too young then to know much about guilt.

Hooter slid his hand down the length of Margaret Leigh's back, and Andrew squeezed the handle of his mug. Guilt filled him. He was the one who had introduced her to the likes of Hooter Johnson. If something happened to her, he was as guilty as sin.

They danced out of his sight, and he stood up

to see if he could spot them. From a distance it looked as if Hooter was trying to get his hand underneath Margaret Leigh's shirt. Andrew had to stop himself from crossing the room and punching him in the face.

He'd always been a peace-loving man. What possessed him to be thinking of using his fists? He sat back on his bar stool and tried to enjoy his root beer. But he kept thinking of Hooter's hands on Margaret Leigh.

He slammed his mug down on the bar and began to make his way across the crowded room. Progress was slow. The Pirates' Den was unusually crowded for a Tuesday night. By the time he got on the dance floor, he'd had to stop and apologize four times for stepping on feet. He searched the crowd. Margaret Leigh was tall, and Hooter was about the size of a hundred-year-old oak tree. They shouldn't be that hard to spot.

"Hey, Andrew. Lost your girl?"

James Johnson and his dance partner, a woman with bleached hair and a permanent pucker, stopped beside him.

"I'm looking for Hooter and the woman he's with . . . tall, dark hair, fair skin, lips that—"

"Hey. That's the woman you were with Saturday night."

"Yes. Have you seen her?"

"She and Hooter skipped out the back door about five minutes ago."

Andrew strode back though the crowd. This time, they parted for him. If he could have seen the look on his face, he'd have known why. He looked as if the hounds of hell were on his trail.

When he got to his truck, he wasted no time wondering what to do. He knew where Hooter lived—in a cabin ten miles from his own. He also knew Hooter's habits. He always took his women to his lair.

Andrew spun out of the parking lot, his tires kicking up gravel.

He was deep in the woods of Boguefala Bottom when his truck died. Andrew made a quick examination of the carcass and decided there was nothing he could do. His cabin was a mile away. He locked his truck and started running.

Margaret Leigh was having second thoughts.

"I've got cold beer in the fridge and plenty of whiskey. What's your pleasure, doll?"

Hooter was leering at her. She pulled her coat around her shoulders and wished she was at her house on Allen Street. She even wished she had accepted Andrew's offer. She wished she was anywhere at all except this dirty one-room cabin in the woods.

"What's the matter? Cat got your tongue?"

Hooter left the refrigerator door open and came around to the kitchen table where she sat, huddled into her coat, miserable and not knowing what to do. He put his hand on her hair.

She kept herself from flinching. Then she squared her shoulders and lifted her chin. She had set out to drown her troubles with a man, and now she had one, such as he was. She was going to be a new woman, even if it killed her. She smiled up at him.

"It was nice of you to offer me a place to stay for the night."

"You've been nice to me; I'll be nice to you." Hooter took her hands and lifted her out of the chair. "That's the way it works, baby."

He dragged her next to his huge bulk and bent

over her. She could smell his breath, a mixture of beer and cigars and stale garlic. His mouth covered hers, and she thought she would suffocate. The taste of garlic almost overwhelmed her. Kissing Hooter was like cuddling up to a pizza with everything on it. She stifled a nervous giggle.

Hooter lifted his head. "Come on, baby, Loosen up."

"I . . . think I'll have that drink, after all."

"Sure thing, doll. What'll it be?"

"Anything. Surprise me."

She stood gripping the back of her chair while he went to the refrigerator. Hooter hummed, and the ice tinkled against the glasses. Then there was a thundering noise at the front door, a battering that practically shook the cabin.

"Hooter. Open up."

It was Andrew. Margaret Leigh sank into her chair, her legs suddenly weak.

Hooter set the glasses on the counter and went to the front door.

"You picked a hell of a time to come calling, boy."

"I didn't have time to send an engraved announcement." Andrew strode into the room, bringing the fresh night air with him. "I came to get my girl."

"*Your* girl?" Hooter scratched his head. "You've staked a claim on this filly?"

"I have." Andrew took Margaret Leigh's arms and lifted her from the chair. Then he pulled her into the protective lee of his shoulder. "Let's go home, Margaret Leigh."

Margaret Leigh was torn between wanting to shoot him on the spot and wanting to hug his neck. She did neither. She took the easy way out. Tomorrow she'd start all over with somebody more refined than Hooter, but right now she'd play along with Andrew. Tipping her head back, she batted her eyelashes at him.

"I'm ready whenever you are . . . darling."

"Now wait a minute." Hooter leaned against the counter and scratched his armpit. "Let me get this straight. She's your girl, but you left her lying around loose, and so she came home with me, bringing her suitcase, I might add. Have I got that right, so far?"

Margaret Leigh freed herself of Andrew's arms and walked over to pat Hooter's face, playing the game to the hilt. She'd seen Tess do it a million times.

"We had one of those silly little lover's quarrels." She pinched his cheek for good measure. "I was mad at him, so I flirted with you."

"Baby, what you did was more than flirt. You teased."

"And you were *so* sweet to invite me over for a drink."

Andrew took a firm grip on Margaret Leigh's arm. "She couldn't have been in better hands, Hooter. Thanks for taking good care of her." He extended a friendly hand to Hooter. The confused man took it. "We'll pick up her car in the morning."

"Shoot. Me and James'll bring it by after a while. That's the least I can do for trying to steal your girl."

"I'll take my own car," Margaret Leigh said.

"And deprive me of your company for one single moment?" Andrew tightened his hold. "We have lots of making up to do . . . darling."

She gave him a look meant to kill, and he laughed. She thought of kicking his shins, but she didn't dare go that far. There was always the

The Publisher of Loveswept® Romances invites you to:

CLAIM
A FREE
EXCLUSIVE
ROMANCE

Lift Here

...PLUS SIX
ROMANCES
RISK FREE

6 ROMANCES FREE

Detach and affix this stamp to
the postage-paid reply card
and mail at once!

NO
OBLIGATION
TO BUY!

THE FREE
GIFT IS YOURS
TO KEEP

SEE DETAILS INSIDE ▶

LET YOURSELF BE LOVESWEPT BY... SIX BRAND NEW LOVESWEPT ROMANCES!

Because Loveswept romances sell themselves ...we want to send you six (Yes, six!) exciting new novels to enjoy for 15 days — risk free! — without obligation to buy.

Discover how these compelling stories of contemporary romances tug at your heart strings and keep you turning the pages. Meet true-to-life characters you'll fall in love with as their romances blossom. Experience their challenges and triumphs — their laughter, tears and passion.

Let yourself be Loveswept! Join our **at-home reader service!** Each month we'll send you six new Loveswept novels **before they appear in the bookstores.** Take up to **15 days to preview** current selections **risk-free! Keep only those shipments you want.** Each book is yours for only $2.09 plus postage & handling, and sales tax where applicable — **a savings of 41¢ per book** off the cover price.

NO OBLIGATION TO BUY — WITH THIS RISK-FREE OFFER!

YOU GET SIX
ROMANCES RISK FREE...
Plus AN EXCLUSIVE TITLE FREE!

Loveswept Romances

```
: : : : : : : : : : :
:                   :
:   AFFIX           :
:   RISK FREE       :
:   BOOKS           :
:   STAMP           :
:   HERE.           :
:                   :
: : : : : : : : : : :
```

Kay Hooper's
**Larger
Than
Life**

This FREE gift
is yours to keep.

MY "NO RISK" GUARANTEE

There's no obligation to buy and the free gift is mine to keep. I may preview each
subsequent shipment for 15 days. If I don't want it, I simply return the books
within 15 days and owe nothing. If I keep them, I will pay just $2.09 per book. I
save $2.50 off the retail price for the 6 books (plus postage and handling, and
sales tax where applicable).

YES! Please send my six Loveswept novels
RISK FREE along with my **FREE GIFT**
described inside the heart! **BR7**   10124

NAME_____

ADDRESS_____APT_____

CITY_____

STATE_____ZIP_____

scary possibility that Hooter might decide to rescue her. She'd save her revenge for later.

As Andrew and Margaret Leigh left the cabin, they heard Hooter on the telephone to his brother. Even after they shut the front door, his booming voice carried through the night.

"James, listen up, now. Shag on out of that Pirates' Den and get yourself over here. My girl's done flew the coop, and I need a card-playing partner."

Outside, Margaret Leigh pulled free of Andrew and leaned against the door. She was glad to be rid of Hooter, but she'd be darned if she'd let Andrew McGill know it.

"You interrupted my evening."

"It was just a small rescue mission. All in a day's work. You can thank me tomorrow."

"Thank you!" She jutted out her chin and started toward her car. "I don't need rescuing, and I certainly don't need you for a keeper."

"You need both." He caught up with her and scooped her into his arms.

"Put me down."

"Why? So you can go back to your lover boy?"

"So I can go to my car, you blackguard." She kicked and flailed.

Ignoring her, Andrew gave a long, low whistle. A black stallion trotted out of the woods. Andrew tossed Margaret Leigh onto the horse's back and mounted behind her.

"A horse! I can't believe it. I'm being kidnapped on a horse."

"Sit still, Margaret Leigh. Do you want to spook him?"

"If you think I'm going anywhere with you on this horse, you're crazy."

"I'm crazy." He pressed his knees into the stallion's sides, and they set off through the woods.

Margaret Leigh felt hysterical laughter welling up inside her. She squelched it by trying to ground herself in reality. The stallion's hooves pounded the earth, and pine trees reached out ghostly arms to her. Overhead, the moon rode high in the sky, bright and yellow as only an October moon can be, lording it over the few stars that decorated the night. And she was headed heaven only knew where on a black horse.

"Take me back to my car."

"Be quiet, Margaret Leigh. I can't enjoy the woods for all your chatter."

"You've ruined my evening. I see no reason why I shouldn't ruin yours."

"I can take you back to Hooter, if that's what you want. He's loud and clumsy and rough around the edges, but he's all man, or so the ladies say. I never figured him for your type, but if that's what you want, I'll be willing to oblige."

She was silent for a while, then she said, "I was just getting ready to leave when you barged in."

He chuckled. "That's what I thought."

They rode the rest of the way in silence. Andrew's cabin came into view. It brought back memories too humiliating to be dwelt upon. Margaret Leigh had been searching in the dark for a way to play the town vamp; she didn't have to search for a way to play the spurned woman. Her anger was fresh and very real. There wasn't much she could do on a horse. She tightened her fists and waited for her chance.

Andrew didn't stop at the cabin; he took Margaret Leigh all the way to the barn. As they passed the kennels, his dogs started howling.

"It's just me, boys," Andrew called. "I'm home. Brought a lady with me, so you fellows be nice."

There was something comfortable and homey about a man talking to his dogs. Andrew's charm crept up on her unaware, so she conjured up the scene in his bed. His charm vanished like dandelions on the wind.

Andrew guided the stallion into the barn, then slid off. "Down you go, lady." He reached up to help her off the horse. On her way down, she kicked him in the shins. "Hey. What's that for?"

"For being an arrogant pirate. For kidnapping me and dragging me through the woods. For depriving me of my lover."

"Is that what this is all about? You're still bent on getting some man in your bed?" He unsaddled the stallion and began to rub him down with angry strokes. "Well, lady, I have news for you. You don't have to prove your desirability to strangers. You're all woman."

"Hooter thinks so. But then, he's all man."

Andrew didn't trust himself to answer as he led his stallion into the stall and latched the door. When he turned around, Margaret Leigh was in a fighting stance, her hands on her hips, her eyes bright, and her hair disheveled from the wild ride through the night.

He stalked her. She backed as far as she could go, and then a pile of hay stopped her. He caught her around the waist. With one powerful movement he had her tightly against his body, her hips pressed into his, her back bowed, and her head bent slightly. He leaned over her, his expression fierce with purpose.

"He's all man, is he?" His voice was dangerously soft. "You thought he'd give you what you want, did you?" He caught her face with one hand, his fingers biting into her tender flesh. She tried to twist away. "Dammit, look at me, Margaret Leigh."

"How dare you touch me."

"I dare." He leaned closer, bringing the scents of pine and leather and hay with him. "Is this what you want, Margaret Leigh?"

His lips slammed down on hers. She locked her teeth together and twisted in his grasp. But she was no match for him. His mouth was seductive, possessive, punishing. It was not a kiss; it was a conquest. And she surrendered. Against her will, she responded to the persuasive power of Andrew McGill.

He knew the moment she surrendered. A chuckle started deep in his chest and, as it made its way up his throat, he lifted his head and turned it loose. His laughter, rich with humor and satisfaction, filled the big barn. The stallion whinnied a reply.

Margaret Leigh was furious. "If you think that proves you're more man than Hooter, you're sadly mistaken."

"I'm far from finished, my love."

He took her lips again. She was embarrassed by the ease of her surrender. Every inch of her body was aware of him. His strength and power sizzled through her until she felt electrified. Her heart wanted to climb out of her chest, and her legs felt weak. Was this what it felt like to want a man, really *desire* him? Nothing in her experience had prepared her for this assault by Andrew McGill. He made her forget everything in her life.

She clung to him, wrapping her arms around his neck and pressing her body close to his. The tenor of his breathing changed, and he lowered her to the hay.

Seven

Their bodies tangled and their breaths mingled. Through his fog of fury, Andrew rationalized what he was doing. He told himself that he was showing her teasing was dangerous. He convinced himself that he was seducing her so that she would know precisely what happened when she enticed men.

Keeping his mouth locked on hers, he reached for her skirt. With one swift move he slid it up her legs. She sucked in her breath and a tremor ran through her. So far, so good, he thought. Let her know the consequences of her actions.

He played his hands over her legs, and suddenly all his reasons changed. Pleasure surged through him. She had the soft satiny skin that he loved so well. She had the delicious curves that made his muscles tighten and his breathing heavy. And yet, she was more than seductive curves and soft skin. She was more than a sex object in the hay. With Margaret Leigh under him, acquiescent, he felt as if he'd never loved before. She made him believe that she was his first.

That wouldn't do. He was teaching a lesson, not falling in love.

With great effort, he separated his emotions from his actions.

"Is this what you want, Margaret Leigh?" He slipped her coat off, then slid her zipper down with the expertness born of experience, at the same time pulling her dress down to her waist. His mouth skimmed down her throat and across one shoulder. "See how easy it is for a man, my love."

Suddenly she stiffened. "Is this an object lesson?"

"Yes." Andrew sat up and drew her dress back over her shoulders. She tried to twist away, but he held her fast, his face grim as he fastened her zipper. "You're no match for a man, Margaret Leigh. You're not strong enough." He smoothed her skirt over her legs, ignoring the way she fought against him. "I'm not going to let you destroy yourself with some fool notion about climbing into bed with the first man who comes along."

She drew her fist back and took a swing at him. He caught her wrist. She glared at him, panting.

"Who made you my keeper?"

"Don't think I wanted to be your knight in shining armor. Slaying the dragons you create is not my idea of a fun-filled evening."

"Nobody asked you to slay dragons."

"I guess it's my great nobility of character. I can't stand to see you throw yourself away on the likes of Hooter."

"I'll find somebody else who is willing."

"Not tonight, you won't."

He plucked her out of the hay with embarrassing ease. She was not a small woman, but Andrew

McGill had a knack for handling her as if she were a hundred-pound weakling. She guessed it must be all that fresh country air that made him so strong. And so sexy.

The last thought came to her unbidden. She studied him as she took the time to regroup. Hay clung to his clothes and his hair. He looked good enough to eat, like something picked fresh from a country garden. Her mouth went dry. It was a new experience for Margaret Leigh, looking at a man and feeling warm inside. And if she thought about his kisses. . . . She wouldn't think about his kisses. She'd concentrate on ways to get away from him.

She was no match for his strength; that was a fact. And he was far too clever to outwit. She'd just have to make him so mad, he'd be glad to see her go.

"I suppose you're planning to tie me to your bed."

His jaw tightened, but he didn't answer. Instead, he scooped her coat out of the hay and stood up. She'd be darned if she'd ask where he was taking her. He stalked out of the barn, bearing her like a sacrifice. The cold wind slapped her in the face, but she refused to shiver.

"It's too bad you can't keep a woman in your bed without tying her up."

"It depends on the woman."

This time she was the one who retreated into icy silence. She lay stoically in his arms, taking pleasure only from the knowledge that he was as disturbed as she. His muscles were rigid, and the usual fluid grace of his walk was replaced by the tight choppy gait of a man walking around land mines.

The dogs created a ruckus when they passed

the dog pen, but Andrew didn't speak to them this time. He marched silently on until he reached the back door of his cabin.

Balancing her in his arms, he opened his screen door and let them in.

"Welcome home." His voice was clipped and icy as he put her down.

"I've had warmer welcomes in funeral parlors." She angrily brushed the hay from her skirt.

"It's a warm welcome you're looking for, is it?" Too late, she saw the gleam in his eye. He had her back in his arms before she could even think about running. She decided her best ploy would be to endure. She tipped her face up and waited for his kiss.

His laughter was quick in coming, but it wasn't a sound of mirth. It was the hollow laughter of a man wrestling with demons. "Do you think I'm going to kiss you again, Margaret Leigh?"

"When you manhandle me, that's usually your intention."

"Not this time, my sweet. What I'd love to do is paddle that pretty bottom of yours." She still had the grace to blush over the fact that a man had actually seen her bottom. To cover her discomfiture, she jutted out her chin and glared at him. "It's mighty tempting, my pet, but I'm not in the mood for more games," Andrew told her.

"You're the one playing games."

"If that wasn't a game with Hooter, what was it?"

"Maybe it was love."

"And maybe I'm the king of England." He picked her up again and carried her through his kitchen, through his den, and down the hallway to his bedrooms. "No, my feisty little minx, the warm welcome I have in mind for you is a good hot bath and big hot toddy."

A bath sounded like heaven, but Margaret Leigh wasn't about to say so.

"You can't make me bathe."

One eyebrow quirked upward over his sizzling blue eyes. This time his chuckle was genuine. "Would you like to bet on that, Margaret Leigh?"

"I'll bathe, but not for you. Only because I want to."

"Now that's my sweet little girl."

"You arrogant pirate."

"You say the nicest things."

He kicked open his bedroom door and marched straight to his bed. He dropped her coat over the footboard and lowered her to the sheets, then he leaned over her.

"Now listen carefully, Margaret Leigh. I'm tired and I'm ready for bed. You're going to get out of your clothes and take a nice relaxing bath while I make you a hot toddy. Then you're going to drink it without protest and go to bed."

She glanced around the room. It was filled with solid furniture and leather-bound books and pieces of Indian pottery. There was a colorful Indian rug on the wooden floor.

"This is your bed."

"Right. You'll sleep across the hall again."

He straightened up and left the room quickly, giving her no time to argue. When he was gone she collapsed. She rolled onto her stomach and buried her head into his pillows. That was her first mistake. His particular smell clung there, the fresh scent of wind in the pines mixed with the heady scent of leather. She sat up quickly, drawing her knees up to her chest and resting her head on them.

She was truly thankful that she'd been spared the night in Hooter's garlic embrace. Maybe she should just give up the fight and go back home. She lay back against the pillows. In the distance she could hear Andrew banging cabinet doors and slamming around the kitchen. A sense of security stole over her, and she relaxed.

The voices came unexpectedly. *Who is my mother? I am. I am. I am.* She clenched her jaws and pressed her hands over her ears until the voices subsided. Anger and determination welled up in her. She got out of bed and went into the bathroom. With quick movements, she undressed and climbed into Andrew's shower. There was only one way to stop the mocking voices. And she'd find that way soon, as soon as she could get out of Andrew's prison.

Andrew stood outside the bathroom door, holding her drink and listening to the sounds of running water. Good. She was taking a hot shower. It would relax her.

He pushed open the door and went inside. She was silhouetted against the shower curtain. He didn't mean to linger, but he couldn't help himself. Seen through the thin layer of semitransparent plastic, her body was lovely. He leaned against the doorjamb and drank his fill. He figured she owed him that much for all the aggravation she'd caused.

She was the most aggravating woman he'd ever met. Furthermore, he was spending time on her as if time were Texas and he owned half of it. He hadn't spent that much time with a female since Trixie, and she'd gone on to win the National Field Trial Championship for him. Tennessee Tiffany Trixie. She'd been a good old bird dog. One of the best.

He smiled. Bird dogs always made him smile.

"Here's your drink."

Margaret Leigh jumped and wrapped her arms around herself. "You're in my bathroom."

"It's my bathroom." He caught one side of the shower curtain and passed the drink through. "Want me to scrub your back?"

"Have you no shame?"

"None." He jiggled the drink. "Are you going to take it, or shall I bring it in to you?"

She shut off the water and snatched the glass out of his hand. He had a sudden hindsight.

"Do you drink, Margaret Leigh?"

"What kind of question is that?"

He smiled. She didn't, and he was glad.

"Don't drink it too fast. And if you need any help getting out of the shower, just give a yell. I'll be right outside the door."

He let the shower curtain drop back into place, then he gathered up all her clothes and left the bathroom. He thought about hanging them in his closet, but that was too chancy. She might find them. He walked to his bed and stuffed them under the covers. A naked woman couldn't go far.

He sat on the edge of his bed and pulled off his boots, a satisfied grin on his face. He'd solved the problem of how to keep her with him without having to sleep in the same bed, tied together. He was only human. He didn't think he could spend another night in bed with Margaret Leigh and come out with his honor and her virginity intact. And he had no doubts whatsoever that she was a virgin. Good grief. Why would a pure woman be moving heaven and earth to give herself to the first man who would have her?

Tomorrow he would find out. If she wouldn't confide in him, he'd go see her Aunt Bertha. She was bound to know.

He was unbuttoning his shirt when she yelled. "What have you done with my clothes?" Her words were carefully spaced. The toddy had done its work.

"They're safe. You'll get them back in the morning."

"What about tonight?"

"Tonight we're going to bed and get a good night's sleep."

"If you think I'm coming out of this bathroom without my clothes, you're mad."

He was delighted. A woman truly bent on seduction wouldn't be worried about a man seeing her without her clothes.

"Come on out. I'll shut my eyes."

"I wouldn't trust you as far as I could throw you."

"Smart woman. I wouldn't trust me, either."

He walked to his closet and pulled out a robe. It was pink and silky, a three-year-old reminder of his affair with Joyce Laton. Joyce had been a fine woman. His parents had harbored high hopes that he might marry her. He'd never even been close. She bored easily, and besides that, she didn't like dogs.

He opened the bathroom door a crack and held out the robe.

"What's that?"

"A robe. I think it might fit you."

"A *woman's* robe."

"That's right."

"You expect me to wear something left behind by one of your floozies."

Her fury shocked him. He had thought she'd be glad for something feminine.

"It's just a piece of clothing. She's not coming back for it."

"How gratifying. I would hate to be rousted out of my sleep by one of your lovers looking for her clothes."

"Dammit, Margaret Leigh—"

"Don't you start, Andrew McGill. You're the one who brought me here. Against my will, I might add."

He pulled the robe back and shut the bathroom door. "You could show a little gratitude. Remember what I saved you from."

"I've gone from the frying pan into the fire if you ask me."

"If you keep shouting, you're going to wake up Christine."

"I'm not shouting."

Women. Why couldn't they be as uncomplicated as dogs? He tossed the robe onto a chair and finished unbuttoning his chamois shirt. Opening the door again, he shoved it through.

"Here. This ought to cover the essentials."

She snatched it from him and slammed the door, barely missing his hand. In a few minutes she emerged, the shirt sleeves dangling below her hands and the tail ending above the knees. He'd never known his shirt could look so sexy.

Her color was high, and she spared him only a brief glance when she marched unsteadily past. "Don't bother to show me the way. I already know."

"Good night, my sweet. Sleep tight."

The slamming door was his only answer. He unbuckled his pants and thought about heading for the shower, then he remembered her purloined clothes. The shower would have to wait. He couldn't risk her searching while he was bathing.

He climbed into his bed, satisfied that he had secured Margaret Leigh for one more night. If he knew her, and he thought he did, she wouldn't dare set foot out of the house wearing nothing more than a man's shirt.

Across the hall, Margaret Leigh stalked toward his guest bed, crawled between the covers, and made her plans. Andrew McGill couldn't beat her. As soon as Hooter and James brought her car, she'd be on her way. She turned on her side and prepared to sleep. She was a light sleeper. The sound of her old car would be her alarm. All she could do was pray that it wouldn't wake Andrew.

Lulled and warmed by the drink, she tucked herself into a ball and drifted into sleep, wrapped in Andrew's shirt.

Bertha heard Margaret Leigh's car. There was no mistaking that rattle. She turned her head and squinted one eye at the luminous dial of the bedside clock. Five A.M. She threw back the covers and crept across the floor. Lord, she was going to an early grave worrying over Margaret Leigh.

She heard the footsteps on the stairs and stood waiting until she was sure Margaret Leigh was in her room, then she followed her. She'd always condemned eavesdropping, but there were circumstances that demanded it, and this was one of them. Without shame, she pressed her ear against Margaret Leigh's door. She was dialing the phone.

"Tess, it's Margaret Leigh. . . . Yes, I know what time it is. . . . No. Nothing's wrong. I guess I'm catching a cold." Margaret Leigh paused to blow her nose.

Bertha wasn't fooled. She stood outside the door, torn between going in to comfort her daughter and staying outside to find out what was going on. Sure of a rebuff, she stayed outside.

"Tess, I called you to get some advice about men. . . . I know you're an expert on the subject. . . . How do you find a nice man to take you to bed? . . . Stop cussing. I'm serious. . . . Well, Harry Cox is the only one I know, and there is a carnival in town. . . . All right. . . . Okay. . . . I don't know if I could do *that*. . . . I'll try. . . . I'm fine, Tess. Stop worrying. . . . I love you too. Bye."

Bertha hurried from her post and crept back down the stairs. Lord, what was happening to her Margaret Leigh?

The first thing Andrew did when he woke up was go across the hall to check on Margaret Leigh. He eased open her door and stuck his head around the corner. The bed was empty. At first he couldn't believe his eyes. He stood in the hall, dumbfounded that his plan had failed. He wasn't accustomed to failing.

He shoved open the door and strode to the bed. It didn't even look slept in. The spread was tucked neatly under the pillows. Don't panic, he told himself. Maybe she was in the kitchen making breakfast.

He hurried through his house. It was small, and it didn't take him long to discover that Margaret Leigh was nowhere on the premises. Where had she gone? Surely not back to Hooter's.

There was one way to find out. On his way to

the phone he glanced at the clock. It was only seven. She couldn't have been gone long.

Hooter answered on the first ring.

"Hooter, this is Andrew."

"How are you, boy? And how's that pretty little filly this morning?"

Relief flooded through Andrew. At least Margaret Leigh hadn't gone back to Hooter. He fished for information. "She's fine, just great. Say, thanks for bringing her car back."

"Shucks, it wadn't any trouble. Me and James was up all night playing cards, anyhow."

"I didn't even hear you when you came. It must have been early."

"Shoot, it was. We left here right after James had beat my pants off. I swear he's cheating."

"What time was that, Hooter?"

"Around four-thirty, I'd say."

"Thanks, Hooter. If I can return the favor sometime, let me know."

"Well, there's that old dog of mine. Possum. I've been wondering what a good trainer like you might do for him."

"Bring him over. I'll do it. Free of charge."

Hooter wanted to talk about Possum's training program, but Andrew found a way to end the conversation, then he hurried outside to feed his dogs.

When he came back inside, he woke a sleepy Christine, fed her, and carried her outside for her toilet. By the time he'd taken his own shower and dressed it was almost eight o'clock. And he didn't even have a vehicle. His stallion was fine for the woods, but it wouldn't do to take him cross-country and onto the streets of Tupelo. There was only one thing to do. He called his brother.

"Rick, I need a favor."

"Can you speak up, Andrew? The girls are yelling about their wet diapers and the boys are trying to get to the moon in their homemade rocket."

"They're too young to build rockets."

"I built it for them. Every boy ought to have a rocket."

Andrew chuckled, then got to the heart of the matter. "I need to borrow your Corvette, and I need to borrow it fast."

"You're never in a hurry. Woman trouble?"

"How'd you guess?"

"I lived through it once myself." Rick stopped talking long enough to give Martha Ann a big kiss as she walked by. There was no telling how long Rick and Martha Ann would have gone on smooching if Andrew hadn't interrupted them.

"Rick. Hey, Rick! What about that favor?"

"All right. Here's what we'll do."

They made arrangements for Rick to come to Boguefala Bottom, followed by his friend and favorite mechanic, Alvin Vinny. Andrew would take the Corvette, and Rick would stay behind to help repair the old pickup. They would swap vehicles whenever it was convenient for Andrew. Martha Ann had her car. Rick was in no hurry to get his Corvette back.

It was nine-thirty by the time Andrew arrived at the house on Allen Street. He climbed out of his brother's snazzy car and hurried up the walk.

Aunt Bertha came to the door.

"Good morning. I'm—"

"I know who you are." She grabbed his sleeve and pulled him through the door. "Come on in."

Andrew followed her into a small sitting room.

She was pale and frazzled-looking, with dark circles under her eyes and white pasty skin. She sank heavily into a wing chair and waved him to another.

"Sit down. I suppose you've come about Margaret Leigh."

Andrew was surprised. He'd thought Aunt Bertha didn't approve of him, and there she was, acting as if he were a hero returning from war.

"As a matter of fact, I have."

"She's safe, for now. She left for the library about an hour ago."

"I'm glad."

"Was she with you last night?"

"Yes." He saw no reason to lie. He was after the truth himself.

"Did anything happen?"

"If you mean did I sleep with her, the answer is no."

"Thank God." Aunt Bertha bowed her head, and tears trickled down her face.

Andrew leaned forward in his chair. "Will you tell me what's going on? Margaret Leigh has been unusually upset these last two days. It's almost as if she'd become another person."

Aunt Bertha lifted her face, wiping at her tears with the back of her hand. Andrew pulled a handkerchief out of his pocket and handed it to her.

"Thanks." She sniffled and wiped her face and blew her nose, then she took a deep sigh and settled back into her chair. "Monday night, at the family dinner, she overheard a cousin talking, telling things she had no business knowing."

"What things?"

"You're going to think I'm awful."

Andrew felt her distress. He left his chair and

knelt beside her, then he took one of her hands in his.

"Miss Adams, I'm not here to judge you . . . or anyone else, for that matter. I'm here to help Margaret Leigh."

Aunt Bertha studied him before she spoke.

"You like her, don't you?"

"Yes."

"Do you love her?"

Andrew didn't know what to say. Love didn't fit into his life-style. It was not something he even thought about. He considered the question carefully. Did he love Margaret Leigh?

"I care for her—very much."

"That's good enough." Aunt Bertha took a deep breath and set about telling Andrew McGill the family secret.

He listened, keeping his astonishment and his opinions to himself. When she was finished, he put his arms around her and comforted her, patting her shoulder and making soothing sounds. Finally she heaved a big sigh and leaned back in her chair.

"Can you help my daughter, Andrew?"

"I can try. I'll be at the library this afternoon when she gets off work, and I'll do my best to help her."

"Thank you." Aunt Bertha patted his face. "I take back everything I ever thought about men who wear leather jackets."

Secure in the knowledge that Margaret Leigh was safe, Andrew returned his brother's Corvette, stayed for a brief visit with Rick and his family, then took his old Ford truck back to Boguefala Bottom.

He spent the rest of the day concentrating on his bird-dog training. By the time he left for the library he was feeling pretty good about Mississippi Rex's staunchiness and style, but he was a bit disappointed in his roading abilities. He had lots of work to get Rex ready for the February trials.

He arrived at the library at four-thirty, thirty minutes before Margaret Leigh's quitting time, but she had already gone. He was suspicious when he didn't see her car in the parking lot. After he went inside and failed to find her, he was furious. He shouldn't have trusted her. Not for a minute. Not after she left his cabin at four-thirty in the morning wearing nothing but his shirt.

He leaned over the checkout counter, controlling his fury and putting on his best smile.

"Do you have any idea where Margaret Leigh went?"

The girl was young and unsure of herself. She chewed on her lower lip.

"Well, I don't know if I should say. I don't want to gossip."

"I'd consider it a personal favor. I promised her Aunt Bertha I'd pick her up today." He shrugged his shoulders. "As you can see, I got here too late."

"Well, she asked to leave early. And I guess I'm not supposed to know this, but I overheard her on the telephone at lunch break talking to somebody named Harry Cox . . . about going to the carnival, I think." She chewed her lips some more.

"Thanks. You're a sweetheart."

Margaret Leigh was standing with Harry Cox in the middle of the midway among all the colored neon and the sawdust, eating a corn dog on a stick and holding the teddy bear she'd won, when she saw Andrew McGill. He was wearing tight jeans and his leather jacket and looking as fierce as Hannibal must have when he crossed the Alps.

She grabbed Harry's lapels, smearing mustard on his shirt.

"Let's go see the sideshow."

"I thought you didn't like freaks."

"I've changed my mind." She tugged. "Come on. Hurry."

Harry Cox wiped the mustard off and did as he was told. Margaret Leigh fidgeted and peered over her shoulder while he bought the tickets, then she practically dragged him to two chairs in a darkened corner of the tent. No sooner had she sat down than she sensed Andrew behind her. She didn't even have to turn around to know he was there. She *felt* him. It was like being thrust into the eye of a tornado.

"Fancy seeing you here, pretty one." She could feel his breath fan her cheek as he leaned close.

She stared ahead, ignoring him.

He leaned closer, whispering in her ear. "I see you've put on some clothes."

She turned her head, then wished she hadn't. She was nose to nose with him, so close she could look into his hot blue eyes, so close she could almost taste his lips.

"Go away," she whispered.

"Never." He nodded toward Harry, who was sitting on the other side of Margaret Leigh, leaning forward to get a better view of the two-headed calf. "Is he your next candidate?"

"Shh. He'll hear."

"You mean he doesn't know. Tell him for me that he's in for quite a treat."

Andrew leaned back in his chair and pretended

to watch the show. Instead he was studying Margaret Leigh. She hadn't changed. She was still holding in her pain, denying the truth, even to herself. But most of all, she was still stubbornly determined to go through with her scheme of self-destruction and revenge.

"Over my dead body."

He didn't realize he'd spoken his thoughts aloud until a man just coming in for the show stopped midway to the chair beside him and said, "I beg your pardon?"

"Nothing. I was just talking to myself."

Eight

Andrew hounded their steps. When Margaret Leigh and Harry left the sideshow, he was two steps behind them. When they stopped to toss pennies into a bottle, he stopped with them. Margaret Leigh tried to lose him in the fun house, but he refused to be lost.

It was obvious to Andrew that Harry Cox didn't know what was going on. Margaret Leigh was flirting shamelessly with him, rubbing her hand along the back of his neck and pressing herself against him in the crowd. The poor man had a dazed look on his face, as if he couldn't quite believe his unexpected fortune.

Andrew bided his time. He wasn't at the carnival to kidnap Margaret Leigh again: he simply wanted to ensure that she stayed out of trouble. Guardian angel wasn't a role he was accustomed to playing, but it had its advantages. There was a certain solitude in being alone in a crowd. The noise served as an incubator for his thoughts, and he didn't have to share them with anyone. Also it was a great way to observe human nature.

He felt as if he were in the back of a theater, watching men cavort and posture upon a stage.

And nobody was playacting more than Margaret Leigh. She was playing the flirt and doing it exceedingly well. Andrew would never have thought he was seeing the same shy woman who had come to his cabin the previous Saturday. Saturday seemed a thousand years in the past.

Harry Cox excused himself and headed to the men's rest room. That's when Andrew made his move. He eased behind Margaret Leigh and took her arm.

"I need to talk to you."

She spun around, her face reflecting the colored lights from the carousel. Behind her came the sounds of music and children's laughter.

"Leave me alone, Andrew. You and I have nothing to talk about."

He touched her face with great tenderness and looked deep into her eyes. "I know why you're running, Margaret Leigh."

She wet her lips with her tongue before speaking. "You know?"

"Yes. Today I visited Bertha Adams."

"You had no right!"

"I care about you. That gives me the right."

"A lot of people used to say they cared about me. It was all lies."

She tried to pull away, but he wouldn't let her go.

"Don't do this, Margaret Leigh."

"Do what?"

"Don't you think I know a game of seduction when I see one. What you are about to do won't solve anything. Let me take you home."

"Home to *Mother*? Home to listen to more of her lies? No, thank you."

"Everybody gets scared about something sometime. Running away won't help. And throwing away everything that has always been precious to you certainly won't help. You'll only regret it later."

"What is this? Amateur psychology?"

"Friendship."

"I don't need you to be my conscience or my guide. Go home, Andrew. Go back to your bird dogs."

She stalked toward the men's facilities, anger and determination in every step she took. Andrew knew of only one way to save her. He strode past her into the men's bathroom.

Harry Cox was standing in front of the stained sink, looking into the cracked mirror and smoothing his hair over his bald spot. Andrew stationed himself behind Harry.

"I'm Andrew McGill, and Margaret Leigh Jones is my woman."

Harry's hands stopped in midair. He moved his mouth once or twice, but no sound came out.

"We had a quarrel, and she tried to get back at me by bringing you to the carnival."

"I didn't know." Harry swallowed hard and his Adam's apple bobbed up and down.

"No harm done. We've patched things up now. I'll take care of her for the rest of the evening."

Harry made one courageous stand. "How do I know you're telling the truth? Maybe you're some stranger who is just trying to cut in?"

"She lives on Allen Street with her Aunt Bertha. Her little dog, Christine, wears pink hair ribbons and doesn't like loud noises. Margaret Leigh doesn't drink, doesn't smoke, and when she goes dancing, she wears a blue taffeta dress. She's inordinately proud of her family, especially Governor Ben Adams, and she's working very hard to make something of herself at the library." He leaned closer to Harry, for the first time in his life using his size to intimidate a man. "Does that about cover it?"

"I guess it does."

"Good. Then this is what we'll do."

He outlined his plan to Harry Cox. Then he went outside to join Margaret Leigh. She was sitting on a redwood bench near the men's room, waiting. Andrew propped his foot on the bench.

"Harry's not coming out."

"I don't believe you."

"I told him I was taking over. He'll stay in there until we leave."

She jumped up, her hands balled into fists. "How dare you." She drew back and swung at him.

He caught her wrist and pulled her close. His jaw tightened as he looked down at her. "I'm not going to let you go through with this."

"With what?" She tried to look the very picture of innocence.

"With getting poor old Harry Cox in your bed."

"Did he tell you that?"

"He didn't have to. I read body language."

She glanced from his face to the men's room, then she sank back onto the bench. "He'll come out. I'm waiting."

"All right." Andrew sat down beside her. "We'll both wait."

They sat side by side, as stiff and cold as two statues in a park. The only difference between them and statues was that the birds didn't come to perch on their heads. Standing on his tiptoes and looking out the bathroom window, Harry Cox almost wished the birds would come. After nearly an hour the two of them were still sitting out there. How much longer would they endure? He studied their faces. Andrew looked as implacable as a mountain, and Margaret Leigh looked as if she could face down a pride of lions.

"He's not coming out, Margaret Leigh."

"That doesn't mean I'm going home with you." She stood up. "This is a carnival. There's bound to be a man around here who is willing to escort me." She set off toward the midway.

Andrew caught her arm and fell into step beside her. "I always did enjoy a country fair. What are we going to do next, my love? Not that sitting on the redwood bench for an hour wasn't fun, but it was a little tame for my tastes. What's your pleasure? The carousel? The Ferris wheel?"

"You've never been able to provide my pleasure." She smiled archly at him.

His jaw tightened as he marched her to the Ferris wheel. Keeping a grip on her arm, he bought two tickets and got in line with her. The line was long and slow moving. During the time they were waiting for their ride, Margaret Leigh began an outrageous flirtation with the muscle-bound roustabout running the wheel.

Andrew was astonished at his capacity for anger. By the time they were strapped in their seats, he was ready to explode. Only his knowledge of why she was acting this way kept him from it.

The wheel started turning, and they began their climb into the air. Margaret Leigh sat as far away from him as possible on the seat.

"Are you cold over there?"

"No. I have my love to keep me warm." She leaned over and blew a kiss at the roustabout as the wheel revolved past him.

"Dammit, Margaret Leigh. Don't you know that what you are doing is dangerous?"

"A dangerous life is far preferable to a dull one."

"You're not going to stop until you get what you want, are you?"

"No."

Andrew unbuckled the seat belt and flung it aside. Then in one swift move, he closed the space between them and pulled her roughly against his chest. Tipping her face up with one hand, he studied her. She was telling the truth. Determination was written in every line of her face. He lowered his mouth to hers.

She struggled against him, twisting her face aside. "What do you think you're doing?"

"I will be your first, Margaret Leigh."

"Never." She glared at him. "Anyhow, you won't be my first."

"You're a virgin."

"How do you know?"

"Because I'm not." She tried to twist away from him again, but he caught her face between his hands. "I'm not going to sit back and let some clumsy fool get his hands on you."

"I wouldn't go to your bed if you were the last man on earth."

"I'll make you change your mind."

He set out to do just that. While the Ferris wheel slowly spun around and the carnival music echoed through the night and the neon lights colored their faces with red and blue and yellow, Andrew McGill courted Margaret Leigh Jones.

He kissed her until her lips ached, caressed her until her body was limp. He was showing her that she couldn't refuse his offer. As he took the sweet nectar of her lips, he kept telling himself that.

And she remained staunch, even as her legs

turned to butter and her heart became a marsh-mallow. Then, when she could no longer deny what was happening to her, when she could no longer keep herself from melting and clinging and blending with Andrew as if they were one, she told herself that she'd put a stop to it when she got good and ready. She'd let Andrew take her all the way to his cabin or wherever he had decided to go. She'd let him undress her and even put her to bed. She'd wait until he was as hot and eager as Tess had said a man could get. And then she'd have her revenge. She'd get up and walk away.

She'd show Andrew. She'd show them all. She didn't need anybody, anybody at all except a face-less stranger to help her make it through one more night. The roustabout on the Ferris wheel had seemed willing. She'd come back to the carni-val, if not later, then the next night or the next. After all, the carnival would be there a week. She'd have a week of wild, mindless passion and hot, raw sex. Then the next week . . . She didn't know how she'd get through the next week, but she'd think of something. Maybe she'd take a cruise somewhere exotic, or maybe she'd pack a bag and get on a bus out of town, or maybe she'd get an offer from the roustabout. Maybe she'd become a carnival follower, a kept woman who didn't have a thing to worry about except keeping the sawdust out of her shoes and a clean sheet on her bed.

She barely knew when the Ferris wheel drew to a stop. Wrapped tightly in Andrew's embrace, she left the carnival. In a fog she got into his truck and allowed herself to be cuddled up against him as he headed out of Tupelo.

Neither of them spoke. They were too busy thinking ahead.

He was making a noble sacrifice. He was going to let Margaret Leigh use him in order to save her from destruction at the hands of a bumbling fool. He was going to be her teacher, her mentor. He would gently initiate her to the ways of love. And when it was over, when she no longer had any reason to wonder what love was like or whether it could block out all her pain, he would be willing to let her stay with him until she could come to terms with Aunt Bertha's betrayal. He'd help her make it through the tough times. And after she had gone home, healed, he'd go back to his bird-dog training and his peaceful Saturday mornings sleeping in the sunshine.

He parked his truck under the trees and looked down at her. Her face was pale in the moonlight.

"We're here, Margaret Leigh. My cabin."

"I guess you bring all your women here."

"No. Only the special ones."

For a moment she pretended she was special, and she was there with Andrew under very different circumstances. She draped her arms around his neck.

"Show me how special." Her eyes closed as she lifted her face to his.

He skimmed his lips across her eyelids and down the side of her cheek. Her head tilted back, and he took her lips once more. He'd always heard that practice made perfect, but he'd never known such perfection as the sweet hot kisses from Margaret Leigh's lush lips. All the fires she'd kept banked for years smoldered to life. The flame of her passion ignited his own.

The kisses became a deep, plunderous prelude to love. If she had been any woman except Margaret Leigh, he'd have taken her in the truck. The intensity of his passion shocked him. How could it be possible that he was rasping for breath and fogging up the windows over a woman he merely intended to save? He drew back from her and tried to see her face in the darkness. It was a pale shadow.

"Margaret Leigh, you can back out. Any time you want to, just say the word, and I'll take you home . . . or wherever you want to go." He traced her cheeks with his fingers as he talked, hoping to calm her, hoping to keep her from thinking he was rejecting her. "It's not that I don't want you. You are a lovely, desirable woman. But I want you to know that you're in control. Tell me no, and I'll stop."

"Don't stop."

Without another word, he got out of the truck and came around to her side. He lifted her out and carried her into the house. It was dark inside. Not a single lamp burned to light their way to his bedroom. His footsteps were loud as he walked down the hallway.

It was the longest walk of Margaret Leigh's life. Wrapped in Andrew's arms and shrouded by darkness, she felt as if she had begun a long journey into a far and mysterious realm. Sounds were magnified for her: Andrew's footsteps hammering on the wooden floor; his breathing, heavy with passion; her own breathing, tight and labored; even the blood pumping through her body sounded loud in the cool, dark quiet of the cabin in the woods.

She clung to the front of his shirt. Feeling his solid flesh underneath grounded her in reality. Otherwise she might have thought she was in the middle of one of her most vivid romantic dreams.

Andrew kicked open his bedroom door. The room was dark except for a patch of moonlight leading from the window to the bed. He lowered her into that circle of brightness. Bending, he traced his hands down the sides of her face.

"You look like you belong here."

She couldn't say a word. Now that she was actually in his bed, she was almost paralyzed. Not with fear, not with anger. She had expected both those emotions. What surprised her was that her paralysis came from anticipation of the unknown.

Andrew leaned closer. The moon spotlighted his eyes, and they were so clear and bright, it almost hurt to look at them.

"I'm going to teach you, Margaret Leigh." His hands traced her face and throat as he talked. "When a man and a woman come together, it is not just a meeting of bodies, it's a meeting of the heart, the mind, and the soul."

His voice was achingly tender. It almost made her forget her plan. He was weaving a spell over her, and she was caught up in the enchantment.

His hands were on her coat buttons. "Love is best when savored. I'm going to savor you, pretty one . . . and teach you to savor me."

She let him slide the coat off and watched while he carefully laid it on a chair. How far should she let him go? How much undressing would it take before she had Andrew in a state of unbridled, uncontrollable passion? Right now he was totally in control. She'd thought sex would be different. She'd imagined that he would push her skirt up and start a frantic exploration of her body. She had thought she could lie back, unfeeling, until the time came to walk out and leave him panting.

She was the one panting. His voice, his eyes, his touch—she was bewitched by them all. He was back again, unzipping her dress and sliding it ever so slowly down her shoulders, and she felt as if her body had suddenly become a violin and Andrew was the maestro. Only his fingers skimmed over her, tracing the lines of her silk slip, and yet every inch of her was vibrating with the music of his touch.

He whispered her name, "Margaret Leigh," ever so softly. She glanced into his eyes and she knew she could not turn away. Not tonight. Maybe not ever. She had to have what he offered under any conditions. It didn't matter that he was only teaching her a lesson. It didn't matter that she had vowed she would never make love with him. Nothing mattered except the moment and the beautiful symphony created by the magic touch of the maestro.

She lifted her arms to him.

"I'm here, Andrew. Take me."

Until that moment Andrew had thought he was rescuing her from the clutches of an uncaring stranger. He had thought the session in his bed would be like so many others, a brief exchange of pleasure between two people. He hadn't counted on his feelings. Suddenly, he knew. He wasn't being noble. He was nobody's hero, nobody's knight in shining armor. He was in love.

The shocking revelation made him motionless. He could do nothing except bend over her, looking deep into her beautiful eyes and wondering when he'd fallen in love and how he could have been so blind.

"Ahh, my love. My sweet." He pulled her up and cradled her in his arms. With his face in her fragrant hair, he crooned to her. "Until you, I never knew the meaning of the word *special*. I never knew what it was like to cherish merely a glimpse of a woman, to watch across a crowded room and feel delight at the sight of dark mahogany hair or the soft curve of a cheek."

He rocked her on the bed, gently, back and forth, her silk-clad body pressed tightly against him. "I never knew that a woman in a blue taffeta dress would fill all my dreams. I thought nothing would ever satisfy me again except the taste of a pair of lush lips."

He was silent for a while, holding onto her and the wonder of being in love. There had never been a moment in Andrew's life when he didn't move with absolute certainty. Now he was filled with doubts. How could he make love to her under the circumstances? She was using him to forget, and she believed he was teaching her a lesson. Ahhh, but how could he let her go? She would consider it another rejection, or worse. And if he declared his love, she'd think it was only a ploy, a part of the game she thought he was playing.

He caught her right hand and twined their fingers together. Then he squeezed very tightly, as if he could never let her go. And he couldn't. He wouldn't. If he refused her now, even if he offered an explanation, she would flee into the arms of another man.

He closed his eyes briefly and prayed for the wisdom to make this night beautiful for Margaret Leigh. She lay against the covers as he stood up and undressed. When he was naked, he settled down beside her.

"Touch me, Margaret Leigh." He took her hand and guided it over his chest. "Know my body."

Her breathing quickened, but she didn't pull back. Her fingers curled into his chest hair, and his heart hammered with a force that surprised him. He had thought there were no surprises left for him in the bedroom. He had been wrong. As her hand moved timidly over his chest, he felt like a schoolboy about to receive his initiation into the joys of the flesh.

"See what you do to me." He covered her hand with his and moved it lower. Her hand trembled then steadied. When her hand surrounded him, she sucked in a sharp breath. He pulsed under her touch. "You have this power, Margaret Leigh. To make me an instrument for your pleasure—" his hands skimmed over the curve of her hips "—and for mine."

He traced the line of her hips again, talking softly all the while. "Let me touch you. Let me know your body."

"Please." Her head arched back, and as the pleasure of being touched spread through her, she began to move.

"Wait, love. There's time." He removed her slip. She had an elegant body, small waist and breasts, long legs and hips molded with feminine curves. He bracketed her tiny waist, then moved one hand upward to span her chest. Her breasts peaked and hardened, pushing against her lace bra. Andrew smiled with appreciation. Margaret Leigh was a woman designed for love. She had an innate sensuality that many women tried for and never achieved.

He felt his own need spiraling out of control. With a great force of will, he held himself in check. If he entered her now, without further preliminaries, he would destroy any chance of truly giving her pleasure.

He moved his hands lightly over her, letting her get accustomed to his touch. When she began to relax, he unhooked her bra and cast it aside. Then he lowered his mouth to hers. She bucked under him and shuddered, then she moaned.

"You are beautiful, Margaret Leigh, every inch of you."

While his lips and tongue toyed with her breasts, he moved his hands over her thighs. He could feel the heat of her through her silk panties. He eased his hand inside her waistband and sought her warmth. She thrust her hips upward, in response.

"Easy, sweet. There's no hurry."

He lifted himself on one elbow and watched her face as his fingers delved gently into her. He saw her initial shock and then her shy smile of pleasure.

"When a man and a woman love, there are many ways to give each other pleasure." His fingers began an expert probing.

Her eyes widened. "Andrew?"

"Do you want me to go on, my love?"

"Plee . . . ease."

For Margaret Leigh, all sensation was centered in that one spot. Slowly, ever so gently, she came to life under the expert manipulation of Andrew's fingers. Feelings she'd never known existed coursed through her. She was both tightly strung and as liquid as hot honey pouring from a jar. Every nerve ending, every muscle, every fiber in her body awakened. Until that moment she'd been a sleepwalker, going through the motions of being alive. With Andrew she was alive, vibrantly, vividly aware of every small movement of his skin against hers, of their mingled scents, lavender and leather, roses and pine.

"Andrew . . . please."

His fingers stilled. "Please stop?"

"Nooo."

Suddenly she tightened, then shattered. She

cried out with astonishment. He sat up, taking her with him, and cradled her in his embrace.

"Ahhh, Andrew."

"There's more, pretty one. Ever so much more." He gentled her, pushing her hair back from her damp forehead, running his hands lightly over her back.

"I want it."

"What do you want, Margaret Leigh?"

"I want . . . everything."

Even now, even after the intimacy they had shared, he needed her consent to continue. He needed to hear her say she wanted him. It was small compensation for unrequited love, but it was enough. For tonight, at least, it was enough.

He lay down, taking her with him. When they were side by side, facing each other, he took her hand and guided it over his body once more. Then he began to stroke her, long, sensual strokes, over her breasts, her hips, her thighs, increasing the tempo, building the tension until she was reaching out to him, moaning.

Her body quickened once more, straining toward him, seeking relief from the fire that burned through her. She was filled with wonder and magic and music. And questions. The single small part of her mind that still clung to sanity, to reality, screamed, *Why?* Why had Bertha Adams warned against sex? How could something so beautiful be considered sin and degradation?

She felt the gentle invasion, the hot silky flesh slipping into her. And through her fog of pleasure, she heard Andrew's voice.

"I don't want to hurt you, Margaret Leigh."

"You can never . . ."

"Shhh." He touched her lips with his fingertips.

"The first time always hurts some, Margaret Leigh."

She was wild with wanting, with needing to know, with the desire to feel him buried deep within her. She thrust her hips upward, straining to enclose him completely.

"Please . . . Andrew . . ."

"I'll be gentle."

Slowly he eased into her, and suddenly she felt the flash of pain. Her back arched, and she stiffened.

"Relax, love. It's over."

"Over?"

Disappointment tinged her voice and showed in her face.

"The hard part." He began to move then, sliding slowly, moving deeper and deeper. "The best part's just beginning."

The beginning was ecstasy. At first she lay under him, acquiescent; then she caught his rhythm. Together they danced to the music that only they could hear. And suddenly the dancing wasn't enough. She felt a tension growing within her, a wild beast in need of taming. Her hands clenched into fists and sweat beaded her brow.

"I know, love. I know." Andrew's lips grazed her cheek, her brow. "Come with me."

"Anywhere."

The music became wild, savage. They plunged to its frenzied beat. Faster and faster they danced, harder and harder until every muscle in their bodies was tight.

"Yes, oh, yes." He closed his eyes and threw back his head.

She cried out his name. Then the release came, sweet and hot. She sagged, and he lay on top of her, panting.

He eased his weight off her, propping himself on one elbow so he could see her face. It was dewy with sweat and the glow of a woman who has just been loved. All the love he felt for Margaret Leigh welled up inside. He wanted to tell her. He wanted to say the words *I love you*. She would never believe him. Not now. Not under these circumstances. He stifled a groan. What had he done? In saving her, he had destroyed himself.

Margaret Leigh took his silence as disapproval. Had she been that bad? Had she been so clumsy, so inept that she had made him speechless? Her eyelids burned with tears, and she shut her eyes tightly to hold them back. She wouldn't compound her sins by crying. What she had considered wonderful, Andrew considered too awful for words.

She swallowed hard, then opened her eyes. "I want to go home."

"Now?"

"Yes. Now."

A heaviness filled Andrew as he rose from the bed. He looked down at her. The pain he saw in her lavender eyes was to much to bear.

"Magg—" He stopped. How could he say, *I'm sorry?* She would misunderstand. She'd think he was sorry he had brought her to his cabin, sorry he'd brought her to his bed, sorry he'd made love to her.

"Yes?" She waited, hoping he would say something to make it right, wishing he would say anything to make what they had done seem beautiful.

His gaze held hers for a small eternity, then he turned away. "Nothing. I'll take you home." He gathered his clothes and started for the door. "Let me know when you're dressed."

The door clicked shut. She clenched her hands

into fists and held them tightly against her eyelids.

"I will not let him see me crying." She rolled over, pressing her face into the pillow. Andrew's scent surrounded her. She inhaled deeply, drawing the essence of him into her soul. She ran her hands lightly over his pillow. *This is where he lays his head. This is where he dreams.* Would he ever dream of her? There would never be another night that she would not dream of him. She stifled a groan.

He had been her first, and he would be her last. Andrew had been right. There was more to a man and a woman than sex. There was love.

Suddenly she felt physically sick. She sat up and hung her head between her legs until the dizziness passed. What had she done? She had used Andrew to forget, and in the process she had destroyed any chance she might ever have had for love.

Her body was heavy as she reached for her clothes. She dressed quickly, anxious to leave the scene of her crime; then she opened the door and peered into the hall.

"I'm ready, Andrew."

There was no response. She left the bedroom and found him sitting in the den in the dark, holding Christine. He looked up when he heard her footsteps.

"I thought you might as well take Christine home too. I'm finished with her training."

"Are you finished with my training, too, Andrew?"

She hadn't meant to say that, but the words tumbled out before she could stop them. He stood up, and even in the dark she could see that he was rigid with anger.

"Is that what you call it, Margaret Leigh?"

"Yes," she said even while her heart denied the lie.

"Then consider your training complete." He strode across the den and handed her the poodle. When his hand brushed against hers, she felt branded. She wanted to catch his hand and hold it to her lips, to beg his forgiveness and understanding. Instead, she accepted her dog in silence.

"You know all there is to know about sex, Margaret Leigh. But love . . . that's a different matter." He started toward the door, calling over his shoulder. "Come. It's getting late."

Nine

She sat scrunched on her side of his truck on the long drive home. The silence between them chilled her to the bone. If it hadn't been for Christine's small, warm body, she figured she'd have frozen to death.

When they arrived at her cottage on Allen Street, they sat in the darkened truck, still not speaking. She sneaked a glance at him. His knuckles where white where he gripped the steering wheel, and a small muscle pulsed in the side of his tight jaw.

A wave of dizziness washed over her again, and she fought the urge to put her head on her knees. Finally he turned to her.

"Are you ready to go inside, Margaret Leigh?"

"Yes."

"You won't leave again tonight?"

She turned on him then, fury written in every stiff line of her face and body. "I'm hardly the kind of woman who hops from the bed of one man into the bed of another."

He almost smiled. Then he got out on his side

of the truck and came around to open her door. She stepped down. He barely touched her elbow as he guided her up the walk and onto her front porch. Bertha had left the porch light burning. The harsh yellow light fell across Margaret Leigh's white face.

Something in Andrew shattered. He slid one arm around her waist and tipped her face up with one finger.

"Make peace with Bertha, Margaret Leigh. Make peace with yourself." She closed her eyes to hold back the tears. "Running away won't solve the problem. It only buries the pain."

She bit down hard on her lower lip. The jolt of pain helped her hold back the tears. "Are you through giving lessons for the night, Andrew?"

"It was never a lesson."

"And I'm the queen of Sheba." She jerked away from him and fumbled with the lock on her front door.

"Let me." He steadied her hand and drove the key home. She pushed the door open and slipped through. "Sleep well, Margaret Leigh."

She pretended not to hear him. She closed the door and leaned against it. He was still out there, standing on her front porch under the glaring light. She didn't have to look through the peephole to see. She *knew* he was there. Her whole body was sensitized to Andrew. She would have sensed his presence in a coliseum filled with ten thousand people.

"It's over," she whispered. "Everything is over."

Christine whimpered. Margaret Leigh scratched behind her ears.

"We're both home now, little girl. I guess we'll have to make the best of it."

She carried her poodle into the kitchen, retied

her sagging ear ribbons, adjusted the night-light, then tucked her into her basket.

"We've both been trained by the master, Christine."

The little dog snuggled into her covers, a doggy smile on her face, and went straight to sleep.

Sleep didn't come that easily for Margaret Leigh. Upstairs in her bedroom, she paced the floor. Finally, exhausted by her restlessness, she undressed, throwing her clothes carelessly over a chair. When she was down to her slip, she ran her hands down the length of her body. It quickened at her touch. She moaned his name in the darkness.

"Andrew . . . Andrew . . . Andrew." In a trance, she walked to her closet and pulled out his chamois shirt. She stuck her arms into the sleeves, hugged it close to her body, and climbed into bed. The sweet remembrance of lying in Andrew's arms washed over her. Her body responded as if he were lying by her side.

All Bertha's warnings about scoundrels sounded in the back of her mind, and she knew they had been false, just as false as the story about being a loving aunt. And the sex itself . . . she had wanted mindless passion and raw coupling. What she had gotten was something else entirely. With Andrew, sex had been sweet and tender, hot and torrid, a beautiful symphony, sweeping and majestic.

And she knew she could never go to Harry Cox or Hooter. She could never go to the carnival and seduce the roustabout. Now she realized how foolish she had been, how childish.

She was thirty-two years old, but in many ways

she was still sixteen. She supposed her cloistered youth had contributed to her naïveté. That and the guidance of her Aunt Bertha.

I'm your mother. She covered her ears to shut out the sound of the voice. Then slowly she took her hands away. She couldn't run from the truth forever. She had to face Bertha. But first she had to tell Tess.

The phone ran at five A.M., waking Andrew from a restless sleep. His first thought was of Margaret Leigh. Fully alert, he picked up the phone.

"Andrew, this is Colter."

Andrew dragged his hand through his hair, wondering why his brother-in-law was calling so early. "Colter, there's nothing wrong with Jo Beth, is there?"

"She's great. I'm great. We're all great." Colter's deep laugh sounded over the line. "We have twins, born twenty minutes ago. My son weighed five pounds, and my daughter weighed four pounds six ounces. She's blond and beautiful, just like her mother."

"Twins! That's fantastic. You're sure everybody is okay?"

"Absolutely. The birth was perfect. You should have seen it, Andrew. Jo Beth and the babies all performed like champs."

"Spoken like a doctor."

"Spoken like a proud father. Can you tell Silas and Sarah? Your parents are getting so old, I thought it would be best if you told them in person. I'll call Rick."

"Wait until the sun comes up. Waking up his children would be like setting loose a hornet's nest in a brass band."

"It's that early? I didn't even notice the time. Tell Silas and Sara we'll be home for the christening as soon as Jo Beth and the babies can travel."

"I will. Give her my love, Colter. Tell her I'll talk to her as soon as she's regained some of her strength."

After Andrew hung up, he dressed and went into his kitchen. He popped the cap on a root beer and sat at the kitchen table in the predawn gloom, drinking it warm straight from the bottle. Brooding was not his style, but now he brooded. Alone in the dark with nothing to comfort him except the familiar sweet taste of root beer, he thought about his lost love. He'd lost Margaret Leigh. The previous night he had destroyed any chance he might have had with her. She would never believe that he had taken her out of love and not out of a desire to teach her a lesson. She wouldn't even believe he'd done it out of a desire to protect her.

He slumped lower in his chair in an uncharacteristically dreary mood, never noticing when the sun came up. If his dogs hadn't howled to be fed, he wouldn't have known how long he stayed in his chair.

Knowing how sensitive his dogs were to his mood, he tried to cheer himself up by thinking about his sister's new babies. He didn't want any anxiety or negative feelings to interfere with his dogs' training for the national field trials.

His dogs wiggled and thumped their tails and licked his hands in joyful greeting. By the time he left their pens, he was almost cheerful. Then he thought about the babies again. That cheered him even more. Thinking of them reminded him of the role he had played in getting Jo Beth and Colter together. "A McGill never gives up," he had told her when she thought she had lost Colter.

"You're darned tootin', a McGill never gives up." His shout startled a squirrel coming down from a nearby oak tree. It gave a squeaky bark and scuttled back up the tree.

Whistling now, Andrew went around to the front of his house where his do-it-yourself flower beds were ablaze with mums. The beds hadn't been weeded in a while, but that hadn't kept them from producing some spectacular blooms. He picked an armful and went into his cabin, still whistling.

There was only one thing to do, and that was to go courting. And this time, he would do it right. First he had to undo all the harm he'd done by taking Margaret Leigh into his bed. Then he had to convince her he loved her. And he could do it. By George, he *would* do it.

But first he would keep his promise to Colter. He had to visit his parents and tell them about their new grandbabies.

By the time he arrived at the little house on Allen Street, the sun was high and his huge bouquet of mums was looking a little bedraggled. He tried to rearrange them.

"Plump yourselves up, boys. We're going courting."

He left his truck, whistling. Bertha came to the door. She had dark circles under her eyes, and she looked as if she had lost ten pounds. She stood in the doorway, clutching the knob so hard, the blue veins stood out in her hands.

"She's not here," Bertha said, even before he could ask.

"She's already at work?"

"No. She called the library director early this morning. She asked for some time off."

"May I come in, please?"

"You might as well. You already know all the family scandal. I guess it won't hurt for you to know the rest."

Andrew squeezed the bouquet and bronze mums tumbled to the floor.

"Has anything happened to Margaret Leigh?"

"I reckon she's gone wild. Staying out all night, coming in looking as if she'd been in some man's bed—"

"She was in *my* bed, and she was there because I love her."

"You promised no harm would come to her."

"I believe the harm was done to her long ago."

"Oh." Bertha's hand flew to her chest. She'd always been able to retreat behind a faulty heart, but there was no retreating from Andrew McGill. He had the look of a man who would tolerate no nonsense. "I *loved* her. I only did what I thought was best for her."

"So did I. It seems we've both made mistakes. I'm ready to correct mine. Can you tell me where she is?"

"Gone to Chicago. She called the airport early this morning." Bertha stood up. "She'll be with Tess. I'll get the address."

She disappeared and came back with a piece of notepaper bearing the address of Tess Jones Flannigan Carson O'Toole. She handed the paper to Andrew.

"Tell her I love her."

"I will."

* * *

Tess and Margaret Leigh were dressed for bed, their feet up on Tess's brass-and-glass coffee table, watching the play of Chicago's lights over Lake Michigan, when they heard the intercom buzz.

"Who is it?" Tess asked.

"Andrew McGill."

Margaret Leigh jumped off the sofa, pulling her robe high around her throat. "Tell him I'm not here."

Tess studied her sister's face a second before she responded into the intercom. "You can come up, Mr. McGill."

"Why did you do that? Tess, what are you doing to me?"

"You're in love with him, Margaret Leigh."

"I never said that."

"You didn't have to. I saw it. I see it."

"I wouldn't fall in love with Andrew McGill if he were the only man on earth."

Tess stood up and put a comforting hand on Margaret Leigh's shoulder. "You don't have to see him if you don't want to, but I want to see the man who stole my sister's heart and her virginity."

"Tess!"

"Look. I consider myself a pretty good judge of men—"

"You don't know squat about men." Anger and fear made Margaret Leigh say things she would never have dreamed of saying a few days before. "Three husbands, and all of them Lord only knows where."

Tess tossed her red hair and laughed. "I do believe you're getting some spunk, sister."

"I told you. We're not really sisters."

"Circumstances don't change who and what we are. We'll always be sisters, no matter who gave birth to you." She put her arm around Margaret Leigh and led her toward the bedroom. "You can hide in here, and I'll handle everything. But I'm warning you, Margaret Leigh, I'm not going to let you hide forever. You've got to face this silly business with Aunt Bertha."

"Silly business!"

"Yes. Silly business. It's no more than a tempest in a teapot. She practically raised us. She loves us. What does it matter whether she's your aunt or your mother? That doesn't change the fact that we were and always have been a family unit." She gave her sister a gentle push toward the bedroom. "Shush, now. I hear your man at the door."

"He's not—"

"Shh . . ."

Tess let Andrew McGill in.

"You must be Andrew McGill." She boldly assessed him. "I approve."

"Margaret Leigh has told you about me?"

"Enough." She took his arm and led him to the sofa. "Sit beside me and tell me how you feel about my sister."

Andrew didn't answer directly. Instead he leaned back and studied Margaret Leigh's sister. She was a stunning woman with exotic green eyes and abundant red hair. She exuded self-confidence in every line of her body. There was an arrogance about her, too, a devil-may-care attitude that told the whole world she'd do as she pleased whether they liked it or not. But she had heart. Andrew was certain of that. Living close to nature deepened his intuition and honed his instincts. Tess Jones Flannigan Carson O'Toole was a woman who loved her sister. He'd bet on that.

He leaned forward so he could maintain eye contact.

"I can tell you that my intentions are strictly honorable." Behind the bedroom door, Margaret Leigh covered her mouth with her hand to stifle her gasp of outrage. "But I'm not going to tell you how I feel about Margaret Leigh. Second-hand communication has a way of causing misunderstandings, and I'm not about to risk any more misunderstandings with her."

"I can assure you that my intentions are honorable as well, Andrew McGill. I would never misinterpret what you said to Margaret Leigh. She's my sister, and I love her."

"Good. But my position is still the same. When I say how I feel about Margaret Leigh, she'll be the first to hear it."

Tess's laughter was full-bodied and uninhibited. And after she had finished, she wiped tears of mirth from her eyes. "I like you, Andrew McGill."

"I like you, too, Tess."

"Not many men stand up to me."

"I don't doubt that."

"Only Flannigan . . ." Her face clouded briefly, then she put on a sunny smile. "She's here, you know."

"I thought so."

Tess's green eyes danced with devilment. "I suddenly remembered that I promised to run down the hall and see Patsy's new wing chairs. You don't mind if I leave you alone for a while, do you?"

Behind the door, Margaret Leigh balled her

hands into fists and muttered, "I'll get you for this, Tess."

"Not at all." Andrew smiled at her. "Take your time."

"I will. Looking at Patsy's new furniture has been known to take *hours*." She belted her robe tighter, gave him a jaunty salute, and left the apartment.

He sat on the sofa, waiting for Margaret Leigh to come out of hiding. He even whistled a tune while he waited.

Margaret Leigh was furious with both of them. She wished he would stop that infernal whistling. Her stomach lurched, and her legs got cramps from standing so still behind the door. She was determined to wait him out.

Fifteen minutes passed, and he was still out there. The whistling had stopped, but she knew he was there. For one thing, she hadn't heard the door shut.

"I know you're not in the kitchen, Margaret Leigh." She jumped at the sound of his voice. "I've checked the bathroom too. I guess that leaves the bedroom." There was a long silence, pregnant with memories; then he started talking again. "I'll be glad to come in there. Do you want this confrontation in the bedroom, Margaret Leigh?"

"Don't you dare come in here."

"You'll come out, then."

"I didn't say that."

"You leave me no choice." She could hear his footsteps on Tess's parquet floors.

"Wait. I'll come out. Just . . ." She paused, thinking of a way to buy time. "Give me time to change."

"Fine."

She didn't want to face him in her bathrobe

anyhow. She took her time going to the closet.
She'd been too upset when she arrived to do more
than flop onto the bed and start talking. Tess had
hung the clothes in the closet every which way.
They were full of wrinkles.

She took down a navy skirt and white blouse,
then changed her mind. She didn't want to face
Andrew McGill looking like somebody's maiden
aunt. She reached for jeans and a sweatshirt,
then decided that was too casual. She didn't want
to give him the idea she was comfortable around
him. Finally she selected a soft, blue-violet wool
dress.

She tried to shake the wrinkles out. It was
hopeless. Reaching onto the top closet shelf, she
pulled down Tess's iron and table top ironing
board and set them up on a flat-topped desk.

Anxiety and the steam from the iron made her
hot. She slipped off her robe and continued her
pressing.

"You look pretty in your slip, Margaret Leigh."
She whirled around, holding the iron out like a
weapon. Andrew laughed. "Is that thing loaded?"

"Get out of this bedroom. I'm not dressed."

"I'll help you."

"Over my dead body."

"Haven't we gone beyond being shy about our
bodies?"

"I'm not being shy, damn you. I'm being
selective."

His jaw tightened and he stalked her. She put
up no resistance when he unplugged the iron,
took it from her, and set it on the ironing board.
Then he took her by the shoulders, forcing her to
look into his face.

"Margaret Leigh, I'm too old and too impatient
for games."

"The games were your idea." She tried to twist away. "Kidnapping me on your horse, ruining my date at the carnival, taking me to your bed."

"You said yes."

He had her there. Not only had she said yes, she'd enjoyed every minute of it. But she'd be damned if she'd let him know.

"You said yes, Margaret Leigh." His voice had grown softer, and he began to caress her bare shoulders. "I told myself I was protecting you. I pretended I was your knight in shining armor, saving you from the real scoundrels of the world." He paused, looking deep into her eyes. "It wasn't like that at all."

"Don't tell me what it was. I know."

"What do you know?"

"I was a diversion for you, a change of pace. A shy little virgin in need of a few lessons."

"Dammit, Margaret Leigh—"

"Well, I'm not that little virgin anymore, thanks to you—"

His mouth slammed down on hers. She clamped her teeth together and tried to resist. But the old familiar langor stole over her, and she was his. She knew it and he knew it. The precise instant she responded, he changed the tone of his kisses. Where he had been fierce and demanding, he became tender and persuasive. Where he had been ruthless, he became passionate.

She laced her arms around his neck and pulled him closer. Her body molded to his.

He lifted his head a fraction of an inch, his eyes gleaming with triumph. She didn't care. She was beyond caring about anything except being in Andrew's arms once more.

"You're right." His voice was soft, silky, seductive, as he caressed her cheeks. "'You're not a shy, scared woman: you're full of fire and passion. And I intend to claim it all."

She fell under his spell. His name on her lips was little more than a sigh. "Andrew."

"Yes, my sweet?"

"I said yes," she whispered. "That night in your cabin, I said yes."

"And now. What do you say now, Margaret Leigh?"

Caught up once more in the heady sensuality of being in his arms, Margaret Leigh could hardly think. Andrew had freed a passionate side of her that she had never dreamed existed. That side of her wanted to say, "Take me. Now. Under any circumstances, under any conditions."

If he had continued kissing her without saying a word, she would have fallen into bed with him and damned the consequences. But he was asking her. What now?

She tipped her head back and looked straight into his eyes. Lying was hard looking into those brilliant blue eyes, but she wasn't about to be the victim again. His or anybody else's.

"Now, Andrew, I say you're dealing with a different woman. A wiser woman. I'm not gullible enough to fall into your bed just to satisfy your male ego."

He crammed his fists into his pockets and clamped down on his control. "Have I already been tried and found guilty, or are you wise enough to give me a hearing?"

"Talk, Andrew. But the minute you touch me again, I'll send you out the door."

"It takes two to touch, my love."

"It only takes one to maul."

Andrew reined in his impatience. Margaret Leigh was a woman suffering great pain. Everything in her life had been turned upside-down by Bertha Adams's revelation. He'd have to remember that.

"This is not about touching." He pulled his hands out of his pockets and held them out to her, palms up. "I promise that I won't touch you again, Margaret Leigh. I will never touch you again unless you want me to, unless you ask me to."

"Don't hold your breath."

"Waiting with bated breath is not my style, Margaret Leigh." He got her robe off the chair and handed it to her. "Put this on. You distract me in that slip."

She took the robe, and their fingertips touched. She jerked her hand back, and he smiled. While she got into her robe, he crossed the room and straddled one of Tess's Victorian chairs. Margaret Leigh smiled at the picture he made; a big, virile male dwarfing the tiny, fragile chair.

"That smile is a good start, Margaret Leigh."

She sat on the edge of the bed, catching the ends of her robe and covering her legs the way she'd been taught. Andrew was enchanted. He'd never imagined that one day he would fall in love and want to settle down. And even if he had, he would never have imagined he'd fall for a woman like Margaret Leigh, a very proper lady with starch in her collar and fire in her veins. He laced his hands together on the carved back of the chair and smiled at her.

"Do you remember the night we went dancing, pretty one?"

How could she ever forget? She took her time answering, not wanting to make any more mistakes with Andrew McGill.

"Yes. I remember."

"I think that's when I fell in love with you."

"Ohhh." She covered her mouth, and her cheeks went rosy.

Andrew considered that a good sign.

"It was the blue taffeta dress, I think. I fell in love with that dress first, and then I fell in love with you."

"You don't have to say things like that to make me feel better. I'm a grown woman. I know that men and women sleep together without being in love with each other."

"I told you: this is not about making love. It's about being in love." He smiled at her again, and she almost believed him. "It took me a long time to discover that I loved you, Margaret Leigh."

She sat very still, not trusting herself to speak. She wanted desperately to believe him, but she also wanted to protect herself from any more pain. It had taken her twenty years to find out Bertha Adams had been lying. She couldn't bear to think of spending twenty years, or even twenty days, with Andrew, believing in his love, only to discover it had all been a lie.

"That's why I followed you to Chicago. You are my love, Margaret Leigh. The woman I want to spend the rest of my life with."

"I'm thirty-two years old, Andrew. And more than half my life has already been a lie."

"Bertha loves you, you know. She asked me to tell you that." He paused, waiting for a response. Getting none, he continued. "Our life will not be built on lies. It will be built on love and trust and friendship and commitment."

She felt tears burn the back of her throat, and she swallowed hard. With her hands clenched tightly together, she faced him.

"How can I ever believe you? How can I know the truth from lies again?"

He started to rise, then sank back into the chair. He had promised not to touch her until she asked. And he would keep that promise.

"I'll make you believe, Margaret Leigh."

"Tess believed. Three times men pledged their love at the altar, till death do us part they all said. It wasn't true. Not any of the three times."

"I wish love came with guarantees, but it doesn't. Do you know anything in life that does?"

"Refrigerators."

He smiled. "Yes, but will they sing love songs and cuddle in front the fire and take long walks in the woods?"

"I think scientists are working on it." She sobered. "Andrew, make me believe you love me."

"I will. I'll take you dancing. We'll dance on the streets if you want to." His face lit up as if he were a little boy watching his first launch to the moon. "We'll go to Orchestra Hall to hear the Chicago Symphony. We'll picnic in Jackson Park and stroll down Michigan Avenue. You love animals . . . we'll go to the zoo."

He stood up, waving his arms with enthusiasm as he talked of his courtship plans. "Tess has an open fireplace . . . we'll pop corn and rent movies and sing silly songs and tell foolish jokes. Or we'll just sit on the sofa with our feet touching and read good books." He gave her his most beguiling smile. "I'll do anything, Margaret Leigh."

"You mean that, don't you?"

He crossed to the bed and stood close enough to touch her. Then he leaned down until his face was only inches from hers. She could smell the scent of pines that was so much a part of him, and she could see the faint shadow of a beard because it was late and he had probably come to Chicago without taking the time to shave. She could see the shadings of gold in his hair and the way his eyes lit at the center when he was excited.

"I pledge my life on it, Margaret Leigh." He reached for her face, and when his hand was so close she could feel its warmth, he pulled back, keeping his promise. "I love you."

She wanted so desperately to believe him. But she didn't. She couldn't. Not yet anyhow.

"If you love me, Andrew," she paused, closing here eyes and praying for courage, "if you love me, go home."

He seemed to have stopped breathing. The animation faded from his face, and it became as cold and still as a corpse. Her heart beat frantically, and she wanted to reach out to him and pull him down to her breast and tell him she was sorry, she didn't mean a word she'd said. But the words hung between them, heavy and ugly, and she couldn't take them back.

He straightened up.

"Do you mean that, Margaret Leigh?"

"Yes. If you love me, you'll go home."

"Did I imagine your response to my touch, pretty one?" His voice was soft and deadly. "Did I only dream the way your body turns to fire when I kiss you?"

"It was no dream." She twisted her hands together. "You elicit a passionate response from me."

"But not love?"

She looked down at the carpet, saying nothing.

"Look at me, Margaret Leigh. Look at me and tell me that you can never love me."

She couldn't. She caught her lower lip between

her teeth as her gaze swung up to his. "You said you would do anything, Andrew."

"I made a promise, and I'll keep it." He turned from her and strode across the room. In the doorway he stopped. Looking back, he said, "I'll keep that promise, but not forever. I won't stay away from you forever."

She covered her mouth with her hand to stifle her groan. Her heart beat so hard, she could hear the hammering. "Andrew," she whispered. But he was already gone.

"I need time," she said. "I can't possibly take on another life until I've straightened out my own. I don't even know who my father is."

But there was no one to hear her.

Margaret Leigh was sitting on the end of the bed when Tess came back to the apartment.

"He's already gone?" Tess flopped on the bed, plumped some pillows behind her back, and rested against the headboard. "I'm disappointed. He looked like the kind of man who wouldn't take no for an answer."

"I sent him back to Tupelo." Margaret Leigh scooted up to the headboard and leaned back beside her sister.

"And he went? Good Lord, and all this time I was thinking how much he reminded me of Flannigan. Flannigan would never have gone away." Tess seemed to have forgotten that he had done just that.

Margaret Leigh wasn't about to remind her. She was happy to change the subject.

"How does he remind you of Flannigan?" Margaret Leigh momentarily forgot her own problems. Mick Flannigan had been Tess's first husband, the love of her life, she'd said the day of her wedding. In the ten years since their divorce, she'd never heard Tess mention him, until tonight.

"They both have a wild streak. I'll bet you anything Andrew McGill sunbathes naked."

"That's exactly what I thought when I first saw him." Margaret Leigh's cheeks colored at the memory.

"Don't you think that's absolutely delicious?"

"I thought it was wicked."

"Hell, Maggy. Aunt Bertha knew less about men than any woman I've ever known. Everything she ever told us turned out to be wrong." Tess was on her favorite subject, men. Relaxed and comfortable, she forgot to be cautious. "Shoot, she probably never had more than one man, and look what a mess she made."

Margaret Leigh drew in her breath, and Tess was immediately contrite. "I'm sorry. I forgot how upset you are by this whole mess."

Margaret Leigh closed her eyes a moment, then looked at Tess. "Don't be sorry. And don't think you have to pussyfoot around the subject of my illegitimacy. I'm a grown woman. It's time I faced the truth like one."

"That's a good start." Tess reached over and squeezed her hand.

"Tess, I have to talk to Aunt . . . hell, she's my mother and I don't even know what to call her."

"Stick with Aunt Bertha. That's sensible."

"You've always been able to take charge of things. Will you come home with me? Will you help me get through this?"

"Give me two days to straighten things out at the club, then I'll leave with you."

Ten

While Andrew's plane was delayed due to fog at Chicago's O'Hare International Airport, he brooded. Love wasn't easy. Heck, he'd known Margaret Leigh wouldn't just fall into his arms, but he'd never dreamed she'd send him away. He was an easy-going, likable sort of guy with his share of charm—or so he'd been told. Where was all that famous McGill charm when he needed it most? For that matter, where was his good sense when he needed it most? He'd had no business promising Margaret Leigh *anything*. He'd just have to think of a new plan. That was all. *Real* courtship was new to him. But he'd learn, and he'd learn fast. He didn't intend to be without the woman he loved forever.

At ten A.M. Tess's intercom buzzed. It took Margaret Leigh a moment to remember that she was in Chicago and Andrew wasn't. She'd asked him to go the night before.

154

She got off the sofa bed and padded into the bedroom to wake Tess.

"Tess." There was no response. Tess was spilled across the bed like a box of paints, her hair a splash of red on the pillow, silk gown a pool of purple, and one high-heeled slipper, hanging precariously from her toe, a bright sparkle of gold sequins.

Margaret Leigh approached and shook her gently by the shoulder. "Tess. Wake up. Somebody's at your door."

Tess snuggled closer to her pillow, her breath rising and falling evenly in sleep. Margaret Leigh had forgotten that it took a ten-piece brass band to wake her sister.

She went back into the den and fiddled with the intercom. She finally found the right button.

"Who is it?"

"Special delivery for apartment ten."

Somebody was sending Tess flowers. Fans, especially men, were always sending Tess flowers.

"You can come up."

When he arrived at the door, the delivery man was almost hidden behind a huge bouquet of pink roses.

"Flowers for Miss Jones."

"She's asleep. Can I sign?"

"Right here."

Margaret Leigh signed for the flowers and carried them back into the apartment. They were fragile and beautiful and fragrant. They filled the whole place with romance.

Tess appeared in the doorway, standing lopsided because she was still wearing only one slipper. She yawned and stretched like a satisfied lioness.

"Was that somebody at the door?"

"Flowers for you."

Tess buried her face in the roses and inhaled. Then she slipped the card from its envelope. "You can send me to Tupelo, but you can't send me away," she read aloud. She looked at her sister, quirking one eyebrow upward. "Shall I go on? These are for you." She turned the envelope over and read the name, confirming what she already knew. "Miss Margaret Leigh Jones."

Margaret Leigh ran across the room and took the card. Her hand shook as she read it. "My heart is with you in Chicago, and it will be with you wherever you are. All my love, Andrew." She looked up at Tess. "He sent flowers."

"I can see that. Men in love often do."

"Do you think he really loves me, Tess?"

"He'd be a fool not to."

"Nobody has ever sent me roses."

Margaret Leigh pressed her face against the flower petals to hide her tears.

Margaret Leigh received a fresh bouquet of roses every day for the next three days. And when she and Tess arrived in Tupelo, a bouquet was waiting for her at her house on Allen Street.

"Did you tell him we were coming home, Tess?"

"No. I believe in letting love take its natural course. He must have inside sources."

They both looked at Aunt Bertha, and she gave an innocent shrug.

"I told you, you can't trust men in leather jackets." Bertha turned away before they could see her smile. "Why don't we have a nice cup of hot tea? There are many things we need to talk about, and I've always found talking easier over a friendly cup of tea." She looked to Margaret Leigh for confirmation.

"Yes. We need to talk." Margaret Leigh hesitated, then went to her mother and put an arm around her shoulders. "The three of us will talk . . . just the way a family should."

For three days after Margaret Leigh came home, Andrew courted from a distance. Every day he sent a small gift—flowers, a box of chocolates, a carousel music box. He gave her time to make peace with her mother; he loved her from a distance.

And on the fourth day he went courting.

Margaret Leigh was in the kitchen baking gingerbread when the doorbell rang.

"Will you get that Tess?"

There was no answer, and then Margaret Leigh remembered that Tess and Bertha had gone to visit Aunt Grace.

"Just a minute." She washed the dough off her hands and smoothed back a strand of hair that had slipped from its pin. "Coming."

Andrew McGill stood on her front porch, the setting sun framing him with splendor. She caught her breath, and stood clutching the door frame.

"Hello, Margaret Leigh."

"Andrew . . ."

"May I come in?" She couldn't seem to force any words around the huge lump in her throat. "I'll take that as a yes."

She backed up as Andrew came into the narrow hallway.

"Don't worry, my sweet. I'm still keeping my promise not to touch you until you want me to."

He came so close that he might as well have been touching her. She could feel his body heat. It seared her from her throat all the way down to her thighs.

"Thank you, Andrew." Her thanks were heartfelt. If he hadn't been keeping that promise, if he had put so much as a finger on her cheek, she'd have taken him by the hand and led him upstairs to her bedroom. She'd have pulled him down onto her brass bed with the crocheted coverlet and begged him to make her feel the music of love again. And damned the consequences.

But that wasn't sensible. She was finished with impulse. No more running from problems. No more trying to deny the truth with matters of the flesh. And the truth was, she loved Andrew McGill, but she was terrified of loving and losing. The way Tess had. The way Bertha had.

She gathered courage by pressing her hands together and tilting up her chin. "Won't you come into the kitchen? I'm making gingerbread."

"My mother makes gingerbread." He followed her into the kitchen. "Hmmm. Smells good. I could eat about fifty gingerbread boys."

"Fifty?" She loved it when Andrew made her laugh.

"Maybe I exaggerated a little. Maybe I can eat only ten."

"You make me glad I baked gingerbread." She backed against the counter for support.

"You make me glad I came." He came close again, so close she could see the golden lights in the center of his eyes. His breath fanned her cheek as he bent down. "Do you know how fetching you look with gingerbread on your face?"

"It's on my face?" She brought both hands to her cheeks. "Where?"

His hand reached out, but he stopped just short of touching her chin. "There." She wiped at the spot, and he pointed to her right cheek. "And there." She rubbed her cheek. "And there." His hand hovered just over her lips.

She circled her lips with her tongue.

"Don't tempt me like that, Margaret Leigh."

"Like what?" Her question was totally innocent.

"With your tongue. You make me want to eat you."

Her cheeks flushed, and she pressed back against the counter.

"Don't worry, sweet. I won't. Not yet, anyhow." He left her quickly, before he yielded to temptation. The chair he straddled offered a little protection, but not much. Having only a spindly piece of wood between him and the woman he wanted was a dangerous situation. He embraced the danger, welcomed the challenge. The prize was worth it all.

"Let me get you some gingerbread. The first batch is still hot." Margaret Leigh was glad for something to do. She knew about baking and serving gingerbread; she didn't know a thing about handling a man like Andrew McGill.

Her hand trembled when she handed him the plate.

Keeping his promise took tremendous will power. "Love is nothing to be afraid of, Margaret Leigh."

"I'm not afraid of you, Andrew."

"What are you afraid of?"

"Loving you."

His hand tightened on the fork. That was the first good news he'd heard, the first indication that Margaret Leigh might be his. "I'm going to show you a different side of love from the ones you've known. I'm going to show you love that goes beyond the physical, love that is almost spiritual, love that endures."

"How can you possibly do that?"

"Do you trust me, Margaret Leigh?"

She sat in a chair facing him before she answered. Then she folded her hands in her lap and looked directly into his eyes. "Believe it or not, you are the person I trust most in the world. You saved me from a horrible fate, even when I didn't want you to. You sent me lovely gifts, even though I never said I loved you." She leaned forward. "Thank you for the gifts."

"You're more than welcome. It was my pleasure."

"And you've kept your promise not to touch me, even though it's obviously hard for you."

"It is. I believe in the power of touch."

"But more than all that, you gave me wise counsel. Because of you, Andrew . . . I've made peace with Bertha."

"I'm glad. She does love you."

"I know that now. While I still have a problem sometimes understanding why she gave me up and why she never told my father of my existence, I'm trying to live with it."

"She told you who your father is?"

"She did, after Tess and I talked her into it. Even though he's dead, she still loves him enough to protect him."

Andrew waited, hoping she would share this part of her life with him.

"He was a politician, a married senator from Georgia. They met when she was working in Washington. His name is Robert Graves Willingham. I am his only child, the child he never knew he had." She pressed her fists hard against her thighs so she wouldn't tremble. "I wonder what would have happened if she had told him about me. I wonder if he would have divorced his wife. I wonder if the three of us would have been a family."

"You can't control the past, Margaret Leigh, but you can control the future."

"I'm learning that." She smiled at him. "Now, what are you going to show me about love?"

"Tomorrow. At seven. I'll pick you up." He popped the last bite of gingerbread in his mouth and stood up, putting the plate on the table behind him.

"I'll be ready." He started toward the door. She called softly, "Andrew."

He turned around. She smiled as she walked toward him. Then, reaching up, she ran her hand tenderly over his mouth. "You have crumbs."

Reluctant to break the contact, she kept her hand pressed over his mouth. He kissed her fingertips, lingering over them, moistening them with his tongue, taking the remnants of dough she had failed to wash away and savoring the peculiar sweetness of her skin.

She stepped back, and he took that as a signal to leave.

"Tomorrow, my love."

And he was gone.

She was ready and waiting for him by six-thirty the following evening, sitting in the den wearing a new dress she'd splurged on, a soft-rose-colored silk. The chair cushions were plumped up and a plate of gingerbread sat on the coffee table. The lamps were turned down low, and she was alone—all Tess's doings. She had insisted that Aunt Bertha accompany her to the movies, although Bertha had protested that she hadn't seen a movie in twenty years and wouldn't even know how to act.

Margaret Leigh answered the doorbell on the first chime. Neither of them spoke. They stood gazing at each other as if looking were a rare privilege and they'd paid a thousand dollars an hour and didn't want to waste a single minute.

Finally, she spoke. Catching the edge of her skirt, she did a curtsey. "Do you like my new dress?"

"You bought a new dress just for me?"

"Yes."

"I've never seen a dress so beautiful, nor a model so exquisite."

She smiled. "Will you have some gingerbread before we go?"

"If you promise to wipe away the crumbs."

"No promises. Not yet, at least."

They sat across from each other in the formal manner of a Victorian couple, behaving as if they had a chaperon peering over their shoulders. Then he escorted her to his old pickup truck. It had been freshly washed for the occasion.

He drove her to a sprawling house set among pines on the west side of Tupelo. During the drive, she hadn't asked any questions, and now, parked in the driveway of the lovely home, she still didn't. Her trust in Andrew was complete.

"My brother Rick lives here. Tonight you're going to meet my family."

"Andrew, I told you I can't make any promises."

"My sweet, as much as I would love to make a formal announcement and introduce you as my bride-to-be, I'm not going to. This visit is for you, and only for you. This is a family gathering. Rick and Martha Ann and their children will be here, of course, and my mom and dad, Sarah and Silas.

Jo Beth and Colter couldn't come because the babies are too young, but you'll see pictures of them."

He put her at ease with his quick smile. "All I ask is that you observe my family and see what kind of love you find."

Sarah and Silas McGill sat on the sofa, side by side, holding hands. They were beautiful as only old people who have loved much and lived well can be. Their spirits shone forth from their wrinkled faces.

Margaret Leigh loved them immediately.

After Andrew made the introductions, Sarah patted the sofa cushion. "Sit beside me, dear. I'll protect you from all the peanut butter and jelly that's liable to come your way during the course of the evening." She reached out and affectionately rumpled the hair of a small, blond boy who giggled and climbed into Silas's lap.

"Grandpa, give me a big hug."

Silas hugged the little boy, then turned to his wife. "Sarah, I don't know who this young fella is, but he seems to like me. Reckon I ought to take his picture?" He nodded toward the camera at his feet.

Sara patted his hand. "That's Michael, your grandson. Remember, Silas? He's one of Rick and Martha Ann's boys."

Silas chuckled. "And gonna be a private eye, just like his daddy, I'll vow."

"Yes, dear. I'll bet he will." Sarah kept patting his hand.

Margaret Leigh found Andrew watching her. She smiled, and he winked, as if to say, what did I tell you?

Rick and Martha Ann breezed in with trays of hors d'oeuvres. Two more little boys trailed along behind them, one making race car sounds and the other riding a make-believe pony.

Martha Ann McGill was a gorgeous woman with black hair, a sassy beauty mark near her mouth, and an infectious laugh, especially when her husband was nearby. And Rick was so much like his brother, Margaret Leigh found herself doing a double take. He had Andrew's blond hair and easy laugh, but didn't have his blue eyes, nor his special brand of wicked innocence, nor his particular sparkle, as if he'd been scrubbed and left in the sun to polish.

All in all, Andrew was more man. Much, much more man. At least, that's what she thought. From the looks of things, though, Martha Ann would give her some argument. It was obvious she thought Rick McGill was the only man on earth. They touched often, his hand on her cheek, her hand on his arm. And the looks they exchanged said what no words ever could: they were still wild about each other, after five years and two sets of triplets, after dirty diapers and winter colds and upset stomachs and taking out the garbage and mopping up spilled orange juice and seeing each other at their grumpiest.

"You must meet the girls." Martha Ann took Margaret Leigh's hand and led her into the nursery. Three white cribs held three sleeping beauties, two with Martha Ann's dark hair and one with Rick's blond. They were sleeping on their stomachs with little fists curled under their pink cherub cheeks and their ruffle-clad rumps saluting the breeze.

"Sarah, Rebecca, and Julia."

"They're angels," Margaret Leigh said.

"Only when they're asleep." Martha Ann went down the row of cribs, tucking a blanket here, adjusting a sheet there, dispensing loving pats on each sweet bottom. "You should be here when they're awake." She paused to laugh. "Or maybe you shouldn't. They're so loud, I think they're all going to be opera singers."

On the way out of the nursery, Margaret Leigh glimpsed a picture on the chest of drawers. It was of a stunning blond woman, a dark, dignified man, and two small babies.

"Jo Beth and Colter and the new babies," Martha Ann explained. "They'll be coming soon for a visit." Her face clouded. "Silas and Sarah are getting old, and he's beyond traveling now. Jo Beth wants to make sure they see their new grandbabies."

Margaret Leigh remembered what Andrew had said at her family gathering: "My family values warmth and fun and spontaneity and happiness." It was beautiful to watch.

Dinner was a lively affair, with the McGill brothers outdoing themselves making everybody laugh. In fact, Margaret Leigh decided that laughter might be the one thing she'd remember most about her evening.

After she and Andrew had said their good-byes and were on their way home, she twisted so she could see his face in the faint dashboard lights.

"Thank you, Andrew. I loved every minute of the evening."

"I'm glad, Margaret Leigh. I wanted you to have a good time."

"I did."

He didn't say, "I told you so." He didn't ask if she saw love in evidence. He didn't push or prod.

He merely kept his eyes on the road and started whistling a merry tune.

And when they arrived at her house, he escorted her to the door with the lightest pressure on her elbow, not really touching but not leaving her to walk in the dark by herself either.

The porch light was on. It cast a yellow glow over them as they stood face to face, saying good-bye but not wanting to.

"Thank you for coming with me." He wanted to say, *Will you marry me.*

"Thank you for asking." She wanted to say, *I love you.*

"I guess I'll be going." He wanted to take her in his arms.

"Yes. You should be going." She wanted to ask him to stay.

"Good night, Margaret Leigh." He started to reach for her then. With the instincts of a natural-born toucher, he curved his hand to cup her cheek. His hand hovered in the air as he gazed down at her. "I do love you, pretty one. And it's the enduring kind. Know that. Always remember it."

She took his hand then and pressed it lightly against her cheek. "I will. I promise."

They stood that way for a while longer, his hand on her cheek, her hand over his, filled with longings and paralyzed by regrets.

"For all the ways I've hurt you, I'm sorry," he said.

"I am too. For all the hard times I've given you. I was very foolish and naïve."

"You were neither. I was overbearing and arrogant."

"You were not. You were generous and protective."

They both laughed.

"If we keep on this way," he said, "we'll have to pin medals on each other." He grinned and waggled his eyebrows at her. "I can think of a few good places I'd like to pin yours."

She blushed.

"Good night . . . again. Sweet dreams, pretty one." He started to leave, then turned back. "Remember . . . when you want me, when you need to be touched, all you have to do is say the word. I'm here for you when you're ready."

He went down the walk, whistling. She could still hear the faint melody as he climbed into his truck. Then the door slammed, and the engine roared to life, and both Andrew and his music drove out of her life.

Andrew's phone was ringing when he got home. It was Rick.

"I like her, Andrew."

"Good. I love her."

Rick laughed. "I guess you're camping on her doorstep, playing that guitar and courting like mad."

"No."

"No?"

"She's the quiet kind who can't be rushed. I'm waiting for her to give me a signal."

"You're waiting? That's not like you. How do you know you won't be waiting forever?"

"Because I know, that's all."

"Let me know if you need any advice. I swept Martha Ann off her feet."

Andrew heard his sister-in-law in the background. "Only because I wanted to be swept, darling." Then he heard kissing sounds. Quietly he hung up. In a few more minutes they would have forgotten that they'd called.

Andrew got his guitar and went to his front porch. It was a balmy night, one of those summer evenings disguised as October. He sat in his rocking chair and struck a chord. Then another. And another. Before long he was playing "All I Ask of You" from *The Phantom of the Opera*.

Margaret Leigh would come to him. Soon. He knew, for he'd roused her sleeping sexuality, he'd stoked the fires, he'd been warmed by them. As he played, the haunting words of the song whispered through his mind.

"Say you love me, Margaret Leigh."

His only answer was a whippoorwill calling from deep in the woods.

Margaret Leigh found Tess waiting up for her.

"How did it go, Margaret Leigh?"

"I had a lovely evening." Margaret Leigh kicked off her heels and sank onto the sofa beside her sister. "I've fallen madly in love with him, and I don't quite know what to do about it."

"I can give you tons of advice . . . some of it's even good." Tess laughed. "Heaven knows, I've had enough experience. What do you want to know first?"

"Well . . ." Margaret Leigh paused, thinking of the many times she'd berated him for living in the woods with nothing but bird dogs and wishing she knew a way to prove to him that she'd been wrong. Then she thought of all the times he'd reached out for her and she'd wanted to be in his arms. But the promise had stood between them, and she hadn't known how to take it all back.

She looked at her sister, bright and beautiful and self-confident. "I thank you for the offer, Tess, but this is something I have to figure out for

myself. If I'm to have a life with Andrew McGill, I
have to learn how to deal with . . . everything by
myself. You won't always be around to tell me
what to do when I make a mess of things."

Tess stood up and stretched. "I have a feeling
that you'll know exactly what to do when the time
comes. 'Night, Maggy."

It took Margaret Leigh three days to figure out
what to do. Fortunately she had a wealth of information at her fingertips—at the library. What did
a man do with bird dogs, anyhow? She found the
answer at the library. What were the National
Field Trial Championships? There were books on
the subject at the library.

She laid her plans and then set about imple-
menting them. And in those three days, she
didn't hear a word from Andrew. The old Margaret
Leigh would have panicked. She'd have thought
that a man like him couldn't possibly be in love
with a woman like her, that he'd said so in a
moment of impulse and had changed his mind.
But the new Margaret Leigh thought of all the
ways he'd shown his love, and she loved him even
more for giving her the time and space she
needed.

When she had everything ready, she went to
Tess.

"I do need to know one thing, Tess."

"Tell me what you need."

Margaret Leigh told her. After Tess had finished
laughing she showed her.

Andrew McGill was sleeping the peaceful sleep
of a man with a clear conscience. He stirred in

his sleep, dreaming that a mosquito was tickling his wrist. He burrowed his head closer to his soft pillow and dreamed he was in a fragrant meadow. He could smell the flowers.

"Andrew."

Now he was dreaming that he heard an angel's voice.

"Andrew."

And the voice sounded exactly like Margaret Leigh's. He sat bolt upright, lifting his hands to rub the sleep from his eyes. There was something attached to his right hand. He blinked, adjusting his eyes to the darkness, and looked at his hand. A golden cord was tied around his wrist, and that cord was attached to another hand, a small, soft, sweet-smelling hand. A smile began to form at the corners of his mouth. Attached to the sweet-smelling hand was a woman, a woman wearing a white silk gown and a smile.

"Margaret Leigh."

"That's my name." She smiled.

"How the devil did you get in?"

"Is that any way to greet a woman in love?"

She leaned forward and kissed him. It was a long time before he wanted to say anything else. He pulled her close, his mouth sealed with hers, her breasts molded against his chest, his free arm wrapped around her waist.

When he finally came up for air, he asked again, "How in the world did you get in?"

"I picked the lock."

"You picked the lock. Good grief, where did you learn a thing like that?"

"I'll never tell."

He laughed. "People go to jail for less."

"Take me prisoner. I'm yours." She nibbled the

side of his neck and rubbed her hand down his thigh.

"There's one little thing standing in my way." He held up their joined hands. "Can we take off the cord that joins us?"

"For now. But the separation will be only temporary. I want to be joined to you forever."

Andrew went very still. He had finally heard the words he'd been waiting for, and he didn't trust himself to speak. All the love he felt for Margaret Leigh welled up inside him, and he got a lump in his throat.

"Do you mean that?" he whispered.

"Now and forever. I love you, Andrew McGill, and if you still want me—"

"If I want you!" He cupped her face and gazed at her as if she were the only woman he'd ever seen. "Margaret Leigh, I want you more than sunshine on Saturday mornings and bird dogs that know how to hold a point. I want you more than old blue jeans washed so many times, they've gone soft and comfortable." He paused, trying to think of all the things he loved most in the world. "I want you more than music played softly on the front porch on a balmy summer evening. I want you more than laughter and buttered popcorn in front of a warm winter fire." His eyes glistened. "I want you now and forever."

For a moment, her own eyes were bright with unshed tears of happiness; then a smile broke through, and finally a soft laugh. "Andrew, does that mean we're going to get married?"

"It does." He chuckled and gave her a formal bow, as formal as a naked man could make. "I couldn't have proposed more nicely myself. I accept, Margaret Leigh."

Grinning, she propped her elbow on her knee

and her hand on her chin and pretended to be deep in thought.

"That's not good enough. Show me, Andrew."

His gaze burned over her as he loosened the silken cord that bound their wrists.

"This could take all night." He tossed the cord to the foot of the bed, and then he began to savor his bride-to-be.

He placed her back against the pillows and traced her with his hands. They skimmed over her shoulders, brushing aside her tiny straps. She shivered as his hands moved lower, outlining the plunging neckline of her gown, leaving goose bumps in their wake. He covered her breasts with both hands, massaging until they were tight and full.

She lay still, watching the play of moonlight in his hair as he continued his erotic exploration. He molded her waist, lingering so long that the heat from his hands penetrated her silk gown and seared her skin. His warmth coursed through her, and she was liquid with need.

"Please, Andrew." She lifted her arms to him.

He covered her with one leg and bent down to kiss her. Between wet, soul-searing kisses, he said, "Love is best when savored . . . and I plan to savor you for a long, long time."

He trailed kisses down the side of her throat, nuzzling all her pulse points while his hand slid up her silk-clad thighs.

"I love you in white . . ." He eased the gown down, exposing her breasts. His hair gleamed gold as he bent over her. "I plan to love you in all the colors of the rainbow." His lips sent shivers through her.

"The sun has never touched you here—" he

paused to savor the spot, then continued, "and here . . . and here . . . but I have . . . and I will."

The gown rustled as he slipped it over her feet and tossed it aside. It formed a pool of white beside the gold silk cord.

Poised above her, taking his weight on his elbows, he studied the face of the woman he loved. "This time, you came to my bed willingly."

"Yes." Her fingertips traced his face. "Oh, yes, Andrew. I'm willing."

"When two people come together out of love, the experience is too beautiful to be described, Maggy."

"Then show me."

And he did. He entered her slowly and with great loving care. When he was fully sheathed, he began to fill her with music and beauty and enchantment and the mystery of a magic too wonderful to comprehend.

Theirs was a sweet and tender joining, an exchange of private vows with only a white silk gown and a gold silken cord as witnesses. And when it was over, he cradled her in his arms, her head resting on his shoulder and his leg draped over her hips.

He kissed her forehead. "Thank you for coming to me."

"Nothing less would have done. I had to show you that I accept you on your terms, Andrew. I love you and want you just as you are."

They lay still a while, enjoying the closeness of two people who have loved long and loved well. There was a small noise, and Andrew lifted himself on one elbow to look at Margaret Leigh. "Did you say something?"

"No." She smiled and rubbed his cheek. "You must be hearing things."

The noise came again, a low pitched whine. He

cocked his head, listening. "If I didn't know better, I'd think I was hearing a puppy."

She chuckled. "I thought he'd be quiet until the morning."

"He?"

She sat up and slipped on her gown, then she reached for his hand. "Come with me, Andrew. I have something to show you."

He grabbed a pair of shorts. "If it's as good as the last thing you showed me, I don't think I can stand it."

"Wait and see."

She led him into his den and flicked on the lights. In the middle of the floor sat a cardboard box, and peeping over the top of the box was a small liver-and-white pointer.

"It's a bird-dog puppy."

She laughed. "I know that, Andrew."

He squatted beside the box and lifted the puppy out.

"He has fine markings, good color." He glanced up at Margaret Leigh. "What's he doing in my den?"

She squatted beside him and began to rub the puppy's head. "He's my wedding gift to you. After all the things I said about your profession, I had to find a way to let you know that I believe in you and what you do."

"He's beautiful. You're beautiful." He leaned over to kiss her, and soon they were wrapped in each other's arms, kissing as if there were no tomorrow. They might have continued if the puppy hadn't protested. He didn't like being squashed.

Andrew pulled back, and Margaret Leigh sat on the floor, drew her legs up, and wrapped her arms around them. "He's not champion stock. I couldn't

afford to get you a puppy sired by champions.
But I know you can train him to be a champion,
Andrew. I just know you can."

Andrew put the puppy back into the box and
led Margaret Leigh to the sofa. Sitting with her
cuddled against his shoulder, he asked her the
question that meant everything to him, the one
he'd almost been afraid to ask.

"It takes space for kennels, space for training."

"I know."

"How?"

"I'm a smart woman, Andrew. I looked it all up
at the library."

"Are you willing to live here with me, in the
woods?"

"On two conditions."

"Name them."

"That you let me get a television. I don't think
I've heard the news until I see Peter Jennings."

"That's a small concession I'm willing to make.
What's the second?"

"That we can add space when the babies start
coming?"

"The babies?"

"You don't want children?" Her face fell. "I
thought . . . well, your brother has six and your
sister has two. . . . and I thought you'd want—"

"Four or five will do nicely." Smiling, he ran his
hand down her thigh. "There's just one thing,
Margaret Leigh."

"What's that?"

"Rick's way ahead. I think we'd better get
started, or we'll never catch up." He lay back on
the sofa, taking her with him. "What do you say
to that, my pretty one?"

She reached for the waistband of his shorts. "I
say we'll never catch up if you don't stop talking."

Epilogue

Boguefala Bottom was in full flower. Redbud and dogwood trees stood side by side, the redbud as flirty as painted ladies at a Saturday-night dance, and the dogwood as shy and blushing as a bride. Violets sprang up in the rich, dark earth, turning their purple faces toward the sun. Oak trees sprouted baby green leaves, and along the sunny hillsides, daffodils and daisies danced in the spring breeze.

Margaret Leigh McGill stepped onto the front porch, her thick dark hair hanging loose around her shoulders. She wore comfortable faded jeans and a soft rosy shirt, and she was wielding a broom and humming.

The bristles sang across the bare boards, kicking up only an occasional spurt of dust. Since Margaret Leigh's advent to Boguefala Bottom, dust and spider webs and mildew and bathtub rings were things of the past.

In the backyard, the dogs were howling their morning greeting to Andrew. Margaret Leigh knew them all by name now—Mississippi Rex and

Sam Pea and Lollipop and Jonas and, last of all, Colonel Leigh, the wedding puppy. She even knew them by their barks. Colonel Leigh was the loudest of all, his voice rising above the din, eager to attract the master's attention.

Margaret Leigh's humming took on a special lilt. She was eager to attract the master's attention, herself. And she knew just how to do it.

"Don't you just love Saturday mornings?" Andrew's greeting preceded him, coming around the corner of the cabin a good half minute before he did. Margaret Leigh propped her broom beside the door and ran down the steps to greet him.

With arms outstretched, she made a flying leap. He caught her, lifted her high, and waltzed her around and around.

"I do. I do. I love every morning with you, Andrew."

"Ahhh, Maggy." He set her on the ground, letting her slide slowly down the length of his body. "How can a man concentrate on bird dogs with a pretty woman like you around?"

"That's what you get, Andrew McGill, for proposing to me."

"If I remember correctly, it was you who did the proposing."

"You said yes."

"So I did." He laughed, then kissed her. "Hmm, that's the way I like to start the day."

"That's the way you started the day an hour ago."

"I like to make ten or eleven starts."

He pulled her into his embrace and kissed her again, slowly this time, savoring the scent of spring breezes in her hair and the taste of strawberry jam on her lips—homemade by his very own wife. Margaret Leigh loved all things domestic. And he was the luckiest man in all the world.

He took his time kissing her, running his hands down the familiar length of her body, feeling her instant response.

"Hmmm, Andrew. How can a lady think with a man like you around?"

"What is there to think about except this?"

He kissed her once more. They clung together until their breathing began to go raspy and their legs began to go weak. From a distance came the *beep-beep* of a car horn and the sound of tires on gravel.

Margaret Leigh glanced toward the road. The rural mail carrier's brown Chevy Nova was coming around the bend.

"Arthur's here," she said.

"He'll be disappointed if we don't give him a show." Andrew bent over her, pressing his lips against hers and keeping one eye on his mailbox.

Arthur Harrison stopped his little car beside the mailbox and tooted his horn once more. Then he leaned far out his window and waved a stack of mail at them.

"If you two lovebirds ain't a sight? I swear, it does an old man good to come out here and see you together. How ya'll doin'?"

Hand in hand, Andrew and Margaret Leigh walked down the short driveway to their mailbox.

Andrew took the mail and shook Arthur's hand. "Top of the world, Arthur, and you?"

"Can't complain. I still got my eyesight and enough teeth to gnaw my ham and peas." His hearty laughter echoed through the woods. He swiveled his head around, appreciating the display of spring color. "It sure is pretty out here."

"We love it." Margaret Leigh squeezed her husband's arm.

"Say, I noticed a piece of mail in there from Grand Junction, Tennessee. Ain't that where you won that championship with one of them dogs of yours?"

"That's the place. Mississippi Rex won in February."

"Well, I guess I better get goin'. The government don't pay me to stop and talk." With a wave of his hand and a blast of his horn, Arthur was on his way, his tires kicking up gravel and dust.

Andrew stood in the dust cloud, searching his mail for the letter from Grand Junction. It was in the middle of the stack, a slim white envelope, official and important-looking.

Margaret Leigh took the other mail from him. "Open it, Andrew."

He tore open the envelope, pulled out the letter, and began to read. Halfway through, he began to smile. The smile became a whoop of joy. He grabbed Margaret Leigh and danced her around.

"Tell me, Andrew. Tell me."

"Mississippi Rex and I have been elected to the Bird Dog Hall of Fame."

"That's wonderful. I knew you could do it."

"Pretty one, you haven't seen anything yet. Wait until Colonel Leigh gets old enough to enter the field trials. Everybody will see a *real* champion then." He took the rest of the mail from her and stuffed it into the mailbox.

"What in the world—"

"The mail can wait. This calls for a celebration."

"I think there's some root beer chilling in the fridge."

"I'm talking about a *real* celebration."

The center of his eyes turned hot as he caught

her hand and led her to his hammock under the trees. Their hands were already undoing each other's buttons as they sank onto the hammock. The lattice screen he'd built the previous fall shielded them from the public.

Snaps clicked and buttons popped and zippers zinged and denim whispered as they abandoned their clothes in a heap on the ground. The hammock tilted crazily until they got their balance.

Holding her above him, Andrew brushed her heavy hair back from her face.

"Remember the day you first came here?"

"And you asked me if I'd ever made love in a hammock?"

"Have you ever made love in a hammock, Mrs. McGill?"

"Ohhh . . . dozens of times, hundreds of times."

He began to nuzzle her neck. "And I always thought you were the kind who would prefer cool white sheets."

"I like them too." She tangled her hands in his golden hair and drew his head to her breasts. "Of course, the hayloft has its advantages."

"Hmmm, sweet . . ." He paused from his pleasures to give her a wicked grin. "How about that quilt by the fireplace?"

"I've been meaning to talk to you about that quilt." Leaning over him, she peppered his face with light kisses, ending with one on the tip of his nose.

"What about that quilt?" He fitted his hands around her hips and settled her in the perfect spot.

"How can a girl think when you do that?" She rocked with pleasure. The hammock seesawed and swayed. Margaret Leigh closed her eyes and threw back her head, reveling in the never-ending joy of loving her husband.

They took their pleasure among the colors and fragrances of spring, with the song of a mockingbird sweet and clear in the morning air. After a long while she lay on top of him, stretched full length, her head on his chest and his hands in her hair.

"You never did tell me about that quilt, Maggy, my love."

"Remember that night we strung Valentines along the mantel . . ."

". . . and popped popcorn over the fire . . ."

". . . and spread that quilt out . . ."

"Hummm, I remember."

"That's when it all happened."

He chuckled. "It sure did."

She propped herself on one elbow so she could see his face. "That's when our baby decided it was time to get started."

"Our baby?" He hung one foot over the side of the hammock and brought it to a standstill. Then he cupped her face and pulled her down, nose to nose with him. *"Our baby?"*

"We're going to have a baby, Andrew."

He closed his eyes and hugged her so close, she could hardly breath. He made small murmuring sounds of pleasure, like the cooing of mourning doves in the barn loft. Then he loosened his hold and tilted her chin up so he could look at her.

"Maggy, do you think it's safe for you to be cavorting in a hammock?"

"I'd say that depended on whom I was cavorting with." She chuckled, then caught his dear face in her hands. "It's perfectly safe, my love, but when I get so big I can't see my feet, I suspect we'll have to act like an old married couple and stick to a nice flat mattress."

"Until then . . ." He ran his hands lightly over her thighs. "Maggy, I think this calls for another celebration."

THE EDITOR'S CORNER

It's a pleasure to return to the Editor's Corner while Susann Brailey is away on maternity leave, the proud mother of her first child—a beautiful, big, healthy daughter. It is truly holiday season here with this wonderful addition to our extended "family," and I'm delighted to share our feelings of blessings with you . . . in the form of wonderful books coming your way next month.

First, let me announce that what so many of you have written to me asking for will be in your stockings in just thirty days! Four classic LOVESWEPT romances from the spellbinding pen of Iris Johansen will go on sale in what we are calling the **JOHANSEN JUBILEE** reissues. These much-requested titles take you back to the very beginning of Iris's fabulous writing career with the first four romances she wrote, and they are **STORMY VOWS, TEMPEST AT SEA, THE RELUCTANT LARK,** and **BRONZED HAWK**. In these very first love stories published in the fall and winter of 1983, Iris began the tradition of continuing characters that has come to be commonplace in romance publishing. She is a true innovator, a great talent, and I'm sure you'll want to buy all these signed editions, if not for yourself, then for someone you care about. Could there be a better Christmas present than an introduction to the love stories of Iris Johansen? And look for great news inside each of the JOHANSEN JUBILEE editions about her captivating work coming in February, **THE WIND DANCER**. Bantam, too, has a glorious surprise that we will announce next month.

Give a big shout "hooray" now because Barbara Bowell is back! And back with a romance you've requested—**THE LAST BRADY,** LOVESWEPT

(continued)

#444. Delightful Colleen Brady gets her own romance with an irresistibly virile heartbreaker, Jack Blackledge. He's hard to handle—to put it mildly—and she's utterly inexperienced, so when he needs her to persuade his mother he's involved with a nice girl for a change, the sparks really fly. As always, Barbara Boswell gives you a sweet, charged, absolutely unforgettable love story.

A hurricane hits in the opening pages of Charlotte Hughes's **LOUISIANA LOVIN'**, LOVESWEPT #445, and its force spins Gator Landry and Michelle Thurston into a breathlessly passionate love story. They'd been apart for years, but how could Michelle forget the wild Cajun boy who'd awakened her with sizzling kisses when she was a teenager? And what was she to do with him now, when they were trapped together on Lizard Bayou during the tempest? Fire and frenzy and storm weld them together, but insecurity and pain threaten to tear them apart. A marvelous LOVESWEPT from a very gifted author!

SWEET MISCHIEF, LOVESWEPT #446, by Doris Parmett is a sheer delight. Full of fun, fast-paced, and taut with sexual tension, **SWEET MISCHIEF** tells the love story of sassy Katie Reynolds and irresistible Bill Logan. Bill is disillusioned about the institution of marriage and comes home to his childhood friend Katie with an outrageous proposition. . . . But Katie has loved him long enough and hard enough to dare anything, break any rules to get him for keeps. Ecstasy and deep emotion throw Bill for a loop . . . and Katie is swinging the lasso. **SWEET MISCHIEF** makes for grand reading, indeed. A real keeper.

Bewitching is the first word that comes to mind to
(continued)

describe Linda Cajio's LOVESWEPT #447, **NIGHTS IN WHITE SATIN**. When Jill Daneforth arrives in England determined to get revenge for the theft of her mother's legacy, she is totally unprepared for Rick Kitteridge, an aristocrat and a devil of temptation. He pursues her with fierce passion—but an underlying fear that she can never be wholly his, never share more than his wild and wonderful embraces. How this tempestuous pair reconciles their differences provides some of the most exciting reading ever!

Witty and wonderful, **SQUEEZE PLAY,** LOVE-SWEPT #448, from beloved Lori Copeland provides chuckles and warmth galore. As spontaneous as she is beautiful, Carly Winters has to struggle to manage her attraction to Dex Mathews, the brilliant and gorgeous ex-fiance who has returned to town to plague her in every way . . . including competing in the company softball game. They'd broken up before because of her insecurity over their differences in everything except passion. Now he's back kissing her until she melts, vowing he loves her as she is . . . and giving you unbeatable romance reading.

Sweeping you into a whirlwind of sensual romance, **LORD OF LIGHTNING,** LOVESWEPT #449, is from the extraordinary writer, Suzanne Forster. Lise Anderson takes one look at Stephen Gage and knows she has encountered the flesh-and-blood embodiment of her fantasy lover. As attracted to her as she is to him, Stephen somehow knows that Lise yearns to surrender to thrilling seduction, to abandon all restraint. And he knows, too, that he is just the man to make her dreams come true. But her fears collide with his . . . even as they show

(continued)

each other the way to heaven . . . and only a powerful love can overcome the schism between this fiercely independent schoolteacher and mysterious geologist. **LORD OF LIGHTNING**—as thrilling a romance as you'll ever hope to read.

Six great romances next month . . . four great Iris Johansen classics—LOVESWEPT hopes to make your holiday very special and very specially romantic.

With every good wish for a holiday filled with the best things in life—the love of family and friends.

Sincerely,

Carolyn Nichols

Carolyn Nichols,
Publisher,
LOVESWEPT
Bantam Books
666 Fifth Avenue
New York, NY 10103

P.S. GIVE YOURSELF A SPECIAL PRESENT: CALL OUR LOVESWEPT LINE 1-900-896-2505 TO HEAR EXCITING NEWS FROM ONE OF YOUR FAVORITE AUTHORS AND TO ENTER OUR SWEEPSTAKES TO WIN A FABULOUS TRIP FOR TWO TO PARIS!

FOREVER LOVESWEPT

FOREVER LOVESWEPT
SPECIAL KEEPSAKE EDITION OFFER
SELECTION FORM

Choose from these special Loveswepts by your favorite authors. Please write a 1 next to your first choice, a 2 next to your second choice. Loveswept will honor your preference as inventory allows.

Loveswept®

_____BAD FOR EACH OTHER   Billie Green

_____NOTORIOUS   Iris Johansen

_____WILD CHILD   Suzanne Forster

_____A WHOLE NEW LIGHT   Sandra Brown

_____HOT TOUCH   Deborah Smith

_____ONCE UPON A TIME...GOLDEN
          THREADS   Kay Hooper

Attached are 15 hearts and the selection form which indicates my choices for my special hardcover Loveswept "Keepsake Edition." Please mail my book to:

NAME:_____

ADDRESS:_____

CITY/STATE:_____ZIP:_____